Belle's Christmas Carol

Books by Michelle Griep

From Bethany House Publishers

TIME'S LOST TREASURES

Of Gold and Shadows

Of Silver and Secrets

NOVELLAS

Belle's Christmas Carol

Belle's Christmas Carol

A Dickens-Inspired Holiday Novella

Michelle Griep

BethanyHouse
a division of Baker Publishing Group
Minneapolis, Minnesota

Published by Bethany House Publishers
Minneapolis, Minnesota
BethanyHouse.com

Bethany House Publishers is a division of
Baker Publishing Group, Grand Rapids, Michigan

Printed in the United States of America

Library of Congress Cataloging-in-Publication Data
Names: Griep, Michelle author
Title: Belle's Christmas carol : a Dickens-inspired holiday novella / Michelle Griep.
Description: Minneapolis, Minnesota : Bethany House, a division of Baker Publishing Group, 2026. | Includes bibliographical references.
Identifiers: LCCN 2026011853 | ISBN 9780764242588 paperback | ISBN 9781493455379 ebook
Subjects: LCGFT: Christmas fiction | Novellas
Classification: LCC PS3607.R528 B45 2026
LC record available at https://lccn.loc.gov/2026011853

Scripture quotations are from the King James Version of the Bible.

Cover design by Dan Thornberg, Design Source Creative Services

Published in association with Books & Such Literary Management, BooksAndSuch.com.

Baker Publishing Group publications use paper produced from sustainable forestry practices and postconsumer waste whenever possible.

26 27 28 29 30 31 32 7 6 5 4 3 2 1

Librarians never get enough love,
so this one's for you, Janea Coker.
Your brilliant smile and love of books
always does my heart good.

And, as always, to the One
who created Christmas in the first place,
leaving behind heaven for the likes of you and me.

ONE

"I will honour Christmas in my heart, and try to keep it all the year."

—Charles Dickens, *A Christmas Carol*

LONDON, ENGLAND
ADVENT SUNDAY, NOVEMBER 1819

Expectant waiting. That's what the Reverend Mr. Thomas had extolled at this morning's Advent service. And Isabelle Beaumont would have none of it.

Belle stepped from the carriage with her father and approached their modest London town house, scowling at the sky. She'd been expectantly waiting for snow, not rain. With Christmas only a month away, she longed for white, fluffy flakes, for it was never too early to don the festive holiday spirit.

Add to list: Petition heaven for snow. Rain is a miserable impostor.

She stomped the damp from her half boots on the mat and stepped inside, already forming a plan to banish the dreariness. If the skies refused to cooperate, then she'd take matters into her own hands.

"Hannah," she called the moment she entered the house.

Father arched a brow while pulling off his beaver hat. The

left side of his mouth quirked up as well, taking his moustache for a ride. "You've not even removed your coat yet. What are you about, calling for Hannah right away?"

"You'll have to wait and see, which was the whole point of today's sermon, was it not?"

She grinned as she hung her bonnet and was working on her coat buttons when Hannah clipped into the front hall. Maid, housekeeper, and butler all-in-one, the petite woman in a massive white apron was a force to be reckoned with, yet as pliable as warmed tallow wax.

"Yes, miss?" Hannah plucked the pelisse off Isabelle's shoulders and gave it a good shake before folding it smoothly over her arm.

"I hope you haven't forgotten it is Advent Sunday. We've coats and shawls to gather for St. Martin's parish, and I mean to help you sort them. If we begin now, we can have everything bundled and ready before evening service."

Add to list: Mend Father's old greatcoat—the one with the worn cuffs.

"Yes, miss, but first you should know I've seated a caller in the drawing room. A solicitor by the name of Mr. Snably. I told him the family was out, but he insisted on waiting."

Hmm. Again with the waiting?

Her father rubbed his jaw. "I am not familiar with the name. Did this Mr. Snably say what his business is with me?"

Hannah shook her head, her mobcap riding low over her brow. "He didn't mention what sort of business, sir, and to be honest, he seemed most interested in speaking with Miss Beaumont."

"Me?" Belle blinked. "What on earth for?"

"There is only one way to find out, daughter." Her father swept his hand toward the drawing room. "Shall we?"

She followed him through the door, where a man rose from the wingback nearest the hearth. The fellow was all spindles and knobs, like a spider come to life. How much time did he spend creeping down the draughty corridors of Westminster Hall in his pursuit of law, his black shoes echoing off the polished marble floors? A lot, judging by his spareness. This was no sit-a-couch given to excessive cups of tea and crumpets.

"Miss Beaumont, Mr. Beaumont." He offered a slight bow. "I am Mr. William Snably at your service, solicitor for Drake, Meekum, and Clive."

"Good day." Belle dipped a small curtsey.

Her father gave a crisp nod. "Welcome, Mr. Snably. Please, make yourself comfortable."

Belle smoothed her skirts as she sat next to her father on the sofa. "I was told you were interested in speaking with me, sir. I hope you are not here to tell me I have somehow run afoul of the law."

"Nothing of the sort, miss." A light chuckle pipped out of him, surprisingly high in pitch, then immediately faded. "But I fear my tidings are not any more pleasant. Of course you are familiar with Mrs. Trumble."

"Why, yes. We shared a cup of tea when I finished my last class of the day at the orphanage on Friday afternoon. She was in quite good spirits, what with planning all the upcoming Christmas festivities for the children." Belle angled her head, curiosity a ripe cherry to be picked—one she couldn't help but reach for. "Why do you ask? Surely she is not in any legal trouble."

"Not per se." Mr. Snably shifted on the chair, lips pinching. "I regret to inform you, Miss Beaumont, that Mrs. Trumble died last evening."

"No!" Her hand flew to her chest. "It cannot be."

Her father's arm wrapped around her shoulder, and she leaned against him, grateful for the support. Mrs. Trumble was gone? Just like that? A blow to the head couldn't have jolted Belle any more than the solicitor's words.

Her father gave her a gentle squeeze. "If you don't mind my asking, sir—and if you'd spare any unnecessary details for my daughter's sake—what were the circumstances of Mrs. Trumble's demise?"

"An accident." Grave lines carved deeply at the sides of the solicitor's mouth. "The dear lady had dined at the residence of one of Haven House's patrons—a Mrs. McCambry, though that is immaterial, I suppose. On her way home, the driver of her cab turned the horses sharply to avoid a collision, and Mrs. Trumble was thrown from her seat. The force landed her out on the cobbles, where she sustained severe internal injuries. She lingered for several hours at a nearby infirmary, but there was nothing the doctor could do. To her credit, however, she remained not only lucid but quite calm as well. Brave woman. I can only imagine the pain she endured."

A sob caught in Belle's throat. She pressed her fingers tightly to her lips to keep a cry from embarrassing them all. Poor Mrs. Trumble. The godly woman did not deserve such a horrific death.

She sank against her father, turning her face into his shoulder. For a while nothing but the sound of her own ragged breathing and the steady tat-tat-tat of rain against the windowpanes filled the silence. Then with a final scrunch of her eyes to stop her tears, she knotted up the grief and stowed it in a corner of her heart to untie later.

Pulling away from her father, she faced Mr. Snably. "Though your news is quite shocking, I thank you for bringing it to me in person."

"That is not all I bring. Mrs. Trumble summoned me in her final hours that I might compose a note for you." He held out a folded paper.

She accepted the missive, opening it with trembling fingers.

Dearest Isabelle,

I had wished to discuss this idea with you in person, but time is short. I shall be brief. It is my desire to leave to you Haven House, for there is no one who loves the children more fervently. Please consider.

Fondly,
Cordelia Trumble

The handwritten words made as much sense as the thin man in a dark suit telling her Mrs. Trumble was dead, so she read it again. And again. Slowly, she shook her head and handed the paper to her father. "I don't understand, Mr. Snably. Did Mrs. Trumble wish me to become the new director?"

"Director *and* owner. You, Miss Beaumont, are the sole heir of Haven House—the building, land, furnishings, and all funds tied to it. The trust Mrs. Trumble established for the orphanage's upkeep is more than ample—enough to secure its operation for decades to come, if properly managed. You will never need to fear for its expenses. Now . . ." He adjusted the cravat at his neck and leaned forward. "Will you accept the charge? For if you cannot or will not, then I must make other arrangements for the facility's management posthaste. I am afraid I cannot leave here today without your answer."

Today? Now? What about all the vicar's talk of waiting on the Lord? How could she possibly make such a huge decision in a trice? And yet . . . the faces of Jack and Anne, Tibby and Pippin, Cricket, Rory, and little Birdie all swam in a swirl of myriad thoughts, making her dizzy. She grabbed on to the arm of the sofa, holding tightly.

Her father refolded the paper. "Is this not rather unusual? Such a note hardly suffices as a legal document. I think we should hear the full details in Mrs. Trumble's will before you go pressing my daughter to commit to something so life altering."

"A fair enough request, sir, and you are correct. The reading of the will generally precedes any imparting of property or personal effects. Yet in this case, there are young lives in the balance. It would not be prudent or wise to leave the orphanage unattended until the reading."

"There are caretakers on the premises. Can they not manage until my daughter has time to collect herself and think upon the situation?"

Hah! Belle stifled an unladylike snort. The caretakers at Haven House were sweet enough folk, hard workers who spoke nary a complaint, but there was hardly a thimble full of common sense between Betty and Joe. "I see Mr. Snably's point, Father. As kind as the Graybills are, they cannot be trusted to maintain things without supervision. For the sake of the children, it is best someone in authority arrive at Haven House as soon as possible."

"Very good, Miss Beaumont." Mr. Snably stood. "I shall meet you there in the morning."

Tomorrow? Her head spun. "But I—"

"I should first like a word with my daughter, sir." Her father rose, pulling her up along with him.

"Oh?" Mr. Snably blinked. "Well, I . . . yes, I suppose you would."

The man's thin legs folded as he sank back into the chair.

Belle followed her father into the front hall. Once he shut the drawing room door behind them, he pivoted, a grim line on his brow. "It is no small thing Mr. Snably asks of you, my dear. Do not feel bullied into making a reckless decision."

Was she being reckless? A flicker of doubt tightened her chest. "You should know I am not so easily intimidated by anyone, not even a solicitor."

"No, you are not." He leaned against the trestle table, planting his hands on the thick oak. "But I do want you to think it through. This will change everything."

That was the problem, wasn't it? Miss Isabelle Beaumont, part-time teacher and daughter of a shipping magnate, would suddenly be—what? A headmistress? The owner of a house of her own? A substitute mother to seven children?

She traced a fingertip along the wainscoting, searching for calm, but her thoughts scattered like leaves in wind. Was she ready? Could she lead?

But then she remembered Cricket's toothy grin when she taught him to read the word *cat*. Tibby's robust hugs. Birdie's silent trust. Could she abandon them now?

Her heart gave its answer before her mind caught up.

She faced her father. "I concede this is a big responsibility, but I am not afraid of it. I love those children, Father. I've worked at Haven House nearly every day these past seven years. It is as much my home as this one. And if Mrs. Trumble thought I was the right person, I owe her the courage to at least try. I can think of no better cause for which to give my time and effort."

He loosened his cravat, a lengthy sigh deflating him. "You have already given much to the noble pursuit of educating children for whom most people wouldn't give a second thought. It is far past time you think of marriage and a family of your own. If you take on this position, your opportunities will not only be limited, I fear they will vanish entirely. Once you take on a task, it engrosses you. You will make no time for personal relationships."

A sliver of fear slid under her ribs. What if he was right? What if she woke in ten years, alone, with only ink-stained ledgers and chalk-dusted pinafores for company?

She blinked the thought away. "You exaggerate, Father." She approached him with a wry grin. "I am not enlisting in a convent. Surely nurturing the next generation is as important as finding a husband."

"That's just it. You have not looked for a husband since you broke the engagement with—"

"Father, please. I am over Ben and have been for ten years now."

"Do you hear yourself, my dear? Ten years. Not that the odious Scrooge fellow deserved you, but still . . ." His hands rubbed up and down her arms. "In all that time you have not found the perfect man you seek because that fellow does not exist."

"Of course he does." She lifted her chin. "I'm looking at one right now."

"Oh, my dear girl." He dropped his hands, a knowing look gleaming in his brown eyes. "You have already made up your mind, have you not?"

He knew her so well. It would be hard to leave him, for he'd been her world since Mother died five years ago. Her heart squeezed. "You're right. I have decided. I intend to move in tomorrow morning and continue Mrs. Trumble's legacy of caring for the children of Haven House. I shall provide them with the best Christmas celebration they've ever had to ease their loss of such a dear woman. I should like your blessing, Father, that is, if you think you can manage here on your own?"

He chuckled. "Don't fret about me, daughter. Hannah will not allow me to wither away on her watch. And so you have my blessing." He lifted his chin, peering down his nose at her. "On one condition, that is."

"What?"

"Promise me you won't get so caught up in the daily management of things that you lose sight of the fact that it is God who is in charge. For you, my darling dear, have a way of carrying the world on those shoulders. You are neither Atlas nor the great Creator. Make use of those He sends your way, and know I am ever at your beck and call."

"Oh, Father." She wrapped her arms around him. "I shall miss you."

"None of it." He pulled away with a wink. "I expect to make frequent visits, you know."

"I am happy to hear it." Though the pain of Mrs. Trumble's death stung unbearably, Belle strode back into the drawing room, determined to do her best to continue the benevolent woman's legacy. "I accept your charge, Mr. Snably, or rather, I should say, Mrs. Trumble's charge."

"Very good, Miss Beaumont." The solicitor rose and clapped on his hat. "I shall meet you at Haven House at nine o'clock tomorrow morning. Good day."

Belle watched him depart, her determination unwavering but a certain amount of unease rising up. She had no doubt she could nurture the sweet children she'd come to love as her own, but the management of day-to-day operations? Well . . . if Mrs. Trumble could do it, so could she. Hopefully.

Add to list: Locate Mrs. Trumble's ledgers. And perhaps a miracle.

Two

> For it is always the person not in the predicament who knows what ought to have been done in it, and would unquestionably have done it too.
>
> —Charles Dickens, *A Christmas Carol*

Rafe Munro glanced skyward as he reached for the front door of his town house, his lips twitching into a wry smile at the gunmetal clouds weeping over London. Some said rain was God's tears. Rafe preferred to think of a late November shower as a holy cleansing, washing away soot and sins. Not tears. God knew his family had shed enough of those for now.

He entered the grand front hall and promptly smacked his shin against the iron leg of a scaffolding stand. Blast. Pain stabbed him to the bone. He clenched his jaw as he yanked off his hat and coat.

"Is that you, Rafe?" His mother's voice floated out from the sitting room.

"It is." He hung his articles on a makeshift row of hooks nailed to the wall, penning a mental note to hound the carpenter to prioritize the coat closet. The end of this renovating madness wouldn't come soon enough for his liking.

Hiding a wince—for surely a bruise was already purpling his leg—he strode into the sitting room and flopped onto the sofa.

Mother rolled her eyes at his indecorum yet didn't pause her needlework. The brightly coloured thread contrasted with her sallow skin. She'd spent far too many days—months, actually—holed up in the house. It pained him to watch the life drain from her stitch by stitch.

"How was service?" she asked.

"Your average fare for the season. Love, hope, peace, joy. Inspiring, as you can imagine, but I confess I should have paid better attention. I was distracted by the enormous feather on Mrs. Capstone's hat that kept bobbing over the pew and tickling my brow." Egads. Even now he could yet feel the wisp of the peacock plume against his skin. He rubbed his forehead. "Mrs. Greenleaf asked after you, as did the vicar."

The sides of her mouth sagged as a melancholy expression shadowed her face. "You know I couldn't have attended. Not today, of all days."

"It's been over a year, Mother. Mourning Jenny will not bring her back."

"She would have been four and twenty today." A lost little girl couldn't have sounded more forlorn.

Rising, Rafe closed the distance between them and squeezed his mother's shoulder. "Jenny will not be forgotten, but it pains me that you are forgetting yourself."

"Don't be absurd." She pulled away from his touch, her needle stabbing the white muslin viciously. "I know exactly who I am."

So did he. A mother whose spirit had been buried in the same grave as her daughter. He crouched before her and gently stilled her hands. "You may know who you are now, but not who you have been. Where is the vivacious Mrs. Rosamund Munro, who ruled the world with a crook of her finger?"

Her chest rose and fell with a huge sigh. "It is difficult to be vivacious when part of my heart died along with your sister and your father. I sometimes wonder how that silly organ keeps its rhythm at all."

"And yet it does still beat, for which I am grateful. Furthermore, I think it is high time you get back to your good works.

I know the boards of several charities have been missing your able guidance. You've told me yourself that Mrs. Trumble has been hounding you with excessive notes of late."

"I cannot go to Haven House." Her head dipped, her voice lowering to a whisper. "I shall see your sister in the face of every orphan."

"Which is no different from seeing Jenny in every room here, and that is part of the reason I began this inconvenient renovation project." He swept his hand toward the freshly sanded floor still waiting to be varnished. "Jenny adored those children and loved every minute of her time at Haven House. Would it not be fitting for you to continue her legacy?"

The steady tap of rain pattered against the glass, the only answer to his question. Not that he'd expected one, but it would have been welcome.

"Perhaps someday," his mother murmured at length. "But not yet."

A grin stretched his lips. "At least you're considering it. That's progress. I shall be lenient on the matter, but one thing on which I shall not be moved is the Christmas Open House. The charities you support count on this measure of good cheer."

She gave a faint smile. "You make it sound as though it keeps all the orphanages running."

"In its way, it does. It's no mere party, after all. The city's charitable set depend upon such gatherings to keep goodwill alive—and the purses that follow it. A bit of music, a glass of negus, and a room full of kind intentions can sustain a dozen causes throughout the winter—orphanages included."

He rose, the heels of his shoes overloud in the sparsely furnished room. He tried not to think of all that yet needed to be done before the gala as he poured his mother a cup of tea from the pot on the side table. "The event is a little under three weeks away. I hope you've been keeping up with preparations."

"There's not much for me to do, really. Invitations are already ordered. I'll pen a menu for the cook and have the staff hang some greens. The real question is, Will the house be ready?"

"It's been a battle with the tradesmen, but yes." Retracing his steps, Rafe offered the cup to his mother. "I am determined that all renovations shall be finished—even if I must take up a hammer myself."

She eyed him as she took a sip, a sudden gleam of life in her blue eyes. "Would that you were as determined to take a wife."

"And that would be my cue to leave." He turned away.

She clutched the hem of his sleeve, halting his retreat. "You cannot run from love forever, my son."

"I'm not." He peeled off her fingers and gave them a gentle pat. "I simply have not found the time, that is all."

"Because you work too diligently. It is high time you took a holiday, Rafe. Promise me you won't work so many hours this Christmas season."

His cheeks puffed as he blew out a long breath. She'd never understand the load he carried. The complexities of his profession, the weight of every client's fate resting on his shoulders. Sometimes he was the only one who stood between an innocent and the gallows. And sometimes—too often—he lost. Not for lack of skill or effort, but because the system itself was flawed. Those defeats had begun early in his career and followed him ever since, each one sharpening his resolve rather than dulling it. But there was no way to explain that to Mother. To her, his career was merely a job, but to him it was a mission—nay, a duty.

One that transcended personal desires.

He tugged at his collar, eager not only to change out of his Sunday suit but to leave this conversation as well. "I appreciate your concern, Mother, but I cannot rely on Harvey to succeed in the Grindlethorn matter unassisted, and the case is to be heard the week of Christmas. Neither I—nor justice—can afford to be negligent when an innocent man's future hangs in the balance."

"It usually does." His mother frowned. "But the fact remains that other barristers take leave."

He arched a brow. "You of all people ought to know I am hardly inclined to dance to society's tune."

"No," she murmured, "you are not." A small smile curved

her lips, then just as quickly twisted into sorrow. "Neither was your sister."

There she went again, bearing the heavy burden of grief. She set her tea aside and resumed her sewing.

Anguish pierced Rafe's heart. He'd do anything to keep that smile on her face. His mother's retreat into grief would kill her if he couldn't come up with something to divert her attention . . . and Christmas might be just the thing. Despite his substantial workload, he'd see that this year would be memorable.

Bending, he pressed a light kiss to the top of her silver-threaded hair. "We shall make this the best Christmas we've ever celebrated."

"That will be impossible without your father and sister, and you know your brother and his family will not be able to attend. They don't return from the Continent until the end of January."

"Good thing I relish an impossible task." He winked as he strode from the room.

Out in the front hall, he gave the scaffolding a wide berth, then trotted up the stairs. Though he was eager for a more comfortable pair of trousers and a lighter-weight coat, he paused in front of his sister's room. At Mother's request, not a thing had been changed since that fateful day a year ago when Jenny had succumbed to pneumonia. Oh, the bed had been remade and the draperies tied back, but other than that he could almost see his younger sister sitting at the desk in the corner, sketching scenery as was her wont. Lamplight always lit the most unique sparks of green and gold in her brown eyes, and her pixie-like, pushed-up nose had been fun to tease her about, especially when she'd stamp her foot in anger. Oh, how he missed her. Everything about her, from the resonance of her alto voice to the way she'd clutch her cross pendant with the pearl at the center—a pearl of great price, she used to say. She had been wind and summer as a child, all sunshine and warmth.

But she'd never been the same after spending half a year at that horrid finishing school she'd talked Mother and Father into allowing her to attend. It had finished her, all right. Turned her into a *proper* woman—distant and ofttimes melancholic. She'd never worn her favorite pendant again, the one that had been so much a part of her. . . .

Now, wait a minute, there was an idea.

He stalked into the room. If he could find that pendant, there was just enough time before Christmas to bring it to a jeweler and have it refashioned into a brooch as a special gift for Mother. Perhaps she'd get out of the house more if she could take a little piece of Jenny with her wherever she went.

He started his search in an ornate trunk near the draperies, but it merely held a collection of women's literary journals tied up with red ribbon, an extra quilt for the bed, and some childhood dolls. He set everything back neatly in order.

Next, he opened the wardrobe, fighting a sneeze from a waft of dust tickling his nose. He ran his fingers along the top of the highest shelf. Nothing. Crouching, he pulled out the bottom drawer and carefully removed shawls, a few pillowcases, and . . . what was this?

Retrieving a small box from the back corner, he opened the lid. Inside was a folded piece of light fabric, the edges embroidered with dainty stitches. Brows gathering, he shook out what appeared to be a little blanket, the sort he'd seen his sister-in-law swaddle about his newborn nephew. Was this a gift Jenny had been working on for him? But no. His elder brother had only recently become a new father. His sister would never have known. So perhaps a little something for her own future, then. But why would she store a baby blanket at the back of her wardrobe instead of inside her dowry chest?

Odd, that.

Frowning, he refolded the fabric, taking extra measure to keep the folds straight, then returned the box.

Her desk, perhaps. That was where she'd spent the most time. The top drawer held charcoal sticks of various lengths, a small knife, and a sealed jar of breadcrumbs beside some squares of cheesecloth to fashion an eraser. The next drawer held blank sheets of foolscap, which he straightened into an orderly pile.

The bottom drawer stuck and took a bit of finagling to move, but eventually it opened to reveal a stack of pastoral sketches. He pulled them out and fingered through the pages, imagining the care she'd taken in forming the trees, the hills, and the small sheep dotting them. Lovely, but no necklace.

He set them carefully inside and shut the drawer—or tried to. The wood scraped and skidded, refusing to close all the way. Bother. He yanked it back out and crouched. Sure enough, there were a few papers jammed at the rear, crumpled now from his manhandling of the rogue drawer. He fished them free. There were only two pages, but as he uncrumpled the paper and smoothed them flat, his breath caught. These were no benign countryside images. The cherubic face of an infant stared back at him. If he didn't know any better, he'd swear it was his brother's child.

But that was impossible.

He sank back on his haunches. Why would Jenny hide a baby's blanket and so lovingly sketch a newborn unless . . .

Air hissed through his teeth as a stunning realization hit him broadside.

The six-month absence five years ago.

The change in her demeanor when she returned.

Her tireless devotion to the work at Haven House.

Great heavens! Had Jenny birthed a child in secret and left it in the care of Mrs. Trumble?

His thoughts took off at a gallop as all the puzzle pieces neatly fit together. Jenny, his high-spirited and remarkably independent younger sister, had always been one to defy convention. Would she have gone so far as to birth a child out of wedlock? Unthinkable . . . and yet the circumstantial evidence could not be denied.

But who might the father be?

His jaw tightened. Jenny had never been without admirers—half the bachelors of London had come calling at one point or another. And yet, to his knowledge, she'd fancied none of them. Not enough to entertain a courtship. Certainly not enough to—

No. That was a mystery for another day. If she'd loved the man, he'd have been in the picture. And if she hadn't, then she'd faced it alone.

Rafe refolded the papers and tucked them carefully into his pocket, mind reeling. What might have driven her to such a desperate act? Fear of scandal was a given. The ruthless judgment of society would have been unbearable for certain. Perhaps she even feared her own family would ostracize her. No doubt his father and brother would have. And Mother would have been beside herself.

Oh, Jenny.

His hands curled into fists, a wave of protectiveness nearly drowning him. As mortifying as it might have been, she should have come to him. Confessed her downfall. He'd have shielded her from the barbs of ugly rumours. As much as he could, leastwise. Yet it was too late for that now.

Or was it?

Jenny might be gone, but if she had birthed a child, that young one was still out there. Somewhere. Had the babe been placed in a proper home? Was he or she treated well? Or ill-used? Perhaps the poor creature yet resided at Haven House. Uncertainty nipped his gut. An orphanage, no matter how well intentioned, was no substitute for a loving family. And if Rafe didn't make it his business to find out, that child could grow up never knowing their true heritage. Or worse, face mistreatment in this cruel world.

He strode from the room, jaw set. He'd stop at Haven House on his way to the Inns of Court tomorrow morning. He owed it to Jenny to investigate, however implausible the notion that she had borne a child in secret was. But he'd have to do so with haste, for to spend too much time on this search might mean an innocent man would soon be transported to the penal colonies of Australia. A sentence as good as death.

And this time, Rafe's conscience would not survive intact.

THREE

> The noise in this room was perfectly tumultuous, for there were more children there, than Scrooge in his agitated state of mind could count.
>
> —Charles Dickens, *A Christmas Carol*

Rain. Again. A smidgeon colder and London could be a Christmas wonderland instead of a grey dungeon. True, it was still only November, yet God was surely big enough not to be constricted by the capriciousness of a silly calendar. Belle emerged from the cab, snapping open her umbrella before her heels landed on the cobbles, wondering at all the possible motives the Almighty might have for holding off snow.

And somewhere, deep down inside, she highly suspected it was for her own edification.

She paid the driver a coin—making sure there were enough shillings left in her reticule to reimburse the dray driver who would later bring her trunk—then she faced Haven House. Painted in shades of sage and cream, it was more of a dollhouse come to life than an institution for orphans. Ornately carved shutters, scalloped eaves, lacy white curtains, and a lacquered front door that matched the ebony of the wrought-iron fence. A little fancy for her tastes, yet it was the sort of home one might drop in on uninvited for a spot of tea and be all the merrier for it.

Add to list: Resist the urge to add personal touches. For now.

So it was odd, then, to see the spidery-legged Mr. Snably pacing on the pea gravel near the front door, the dip of his brow as dark as his black coat and umbrella. He strode toward her as she shut the gate.

"Good morning, Miss Beaumont."

"Good morning, Mr. Snably. Surely you are not locked out?"

"No, the keys are right here." He held up a brass ring while casting a distracted glance at the orphanage.

"Then ought we not conduct our business inside? It is raining, after all." Emphasizing her point, she jiggled her umbrella, letting loose a cascade of droplets.

"Hmm?" His gaze drifted back to her. "Oh yes. Or I mean no. Here will do just fine. I am wondering, Miss Beaumont, now that you've had a chance to sleep on your decision, if you have changed your mind? This is quite a big undertaking for such a gentlewoman as yourself. There is no shame in saying no to Mrs. Trumble's inheritance. In fact, I think the best course of action would be for me to find a replacement for you posthaste." He pocketed the keys and strode through the gate, his shoes grinding the gravel.

What on earth?

"Hold on, there, Mr. Snably." Gathering her hem, Belle chased after him, gaining his side while he hailed an oncoming cab. "I have most certainly not changed my mind, and I fail to understand your rather peculiar behaviour."

After flagging down an oncoming hackney, he turned to her. "The truth is, Miss Beaumont, I regret I didn't give you enough time for consideration of the immense undertaking you will be shouldering. I myself didn't realize the enormity of the situation until this morning."

She cocked her head. "Why? What has happened?"

"I had no idea of the building's current state. Apparently there was a small fire last evening. A chimney that ought to have been cleaned more thoroughly ignited in the main hall."

"Fire!" Her eyes widened. "Are the children all right?"

"They are unscathed, or so I was told by the Graybills."

"Thank God!"

"Even so, their behaviour leaves much to be desired. I cannot expect to saddle you with such a life-changing commitment."

Had the man never been inside an orphanage until today? "If you don't mind me asking, Mr. Snably, do you have children of your own?"

"I am not married, Miss Beaumont, so no."

"Then I think it fair to say you may simply not be familiar with childish conduct. I assure you that after working here these past seven years, I am fully aware of how lively the children can be. Furthermore, I suspect they are out of sorts due to the loss of Mrs. Trumble. The sooner I settle in, the sooner they shall settle as well. So, if you would hand over the keys, I shall begin at once to righting things inside Haven House." She held out her hand, and without the shelter of the umbrella, her gloves were promptly and thoroughly dampened.

He glanced at her fingers. "Only if you are certain, Miss Beaumont."

"Quite."

He dropped the brass ring onto her palm, metal jingling at the landing, then gazed earnestly at her with those dark button eyes of his. "There you are, but do not let it be said I haven't fully advised you on what a formidable task you are assuming."

She grinned. "I will not take you to court, if that is your worry."

"That, Miss Beaumont, is the least of my concerns. I shall be in contact. Good day." He dipped his head, then yanked open the door of a black cab that had barely come to a stop.

Tucking the keys into her coat pocket, Belle strode up the gravel walkway to the first day of her new life. And yet her sure steps faltered. Mrs. Trumble should have been here to greet her with her ever-present smile. The thought hit her with such a sudden force she pressed a gloved hand to her mouth. This place might be hers now, but it would never be the same without that dear woman manning the helm. She gave herself a heartbeat to breathe through the ache.

Then squared her shoulders and turned the key.

Inside, she immediately dropped her umbrella and flung her fingers to her nose. The acrid stink of smoke hung thick on the air, mingling with the noxious odour of charred wood. She glanced at the source—the main hall, opening off the receiving area to her left. Small fire, indeed!

Advancing with tentative steps, she sucked in an audible breath as her gaze swept the room and landed on the far side, where black destruction spread outward from the hearth. Intense heat had cracked the brickwork, where burning embers must have escaped and set the wooden mantel ablaze. The nearest floorboards were scorched to brittle remnants. Furniture closest to the fireplace was naught but ebony corpses, their blackened bones scattered about. One window was shattered, sooty glass strewn atop the planks in dangerous shards. Heat had bubbled the paint on the walls, but thankfully the overhead wooden beams—while singed—were yet intact. A mercy, that. But still . . .

Oh dear.

Belle slapped a hand to her heart, grateful the blazing monster had somehow been contained to this room, yet at the same time, she was overwhelmed by the damage. Extensive repairs would be required—repairs that would be hard-pressed to be finished by Christmas. Her stomach knotted into a tight ball. So much for making the merriest holiday ever for the children.

Add to list: Rebuild half the front room as soon as possible. Perhaps with stone. Or iron. Or prayer.

Shrieks of laughter rang out from the dining room down the corridor. She'd have to make a full assessment of the fire damage later.

"Betty? Joe?" she called as she strode along the passageway. Neither person answered. Nor were the Graybills in the dining room.

But the children were—and quite off the tether, at that.

Twelve-year-old Jack chased Anne and the twins—Tibby and Pippin—around the table. Tibby squealed the loudest, her red curls flying. Cricket—in all his five-year-old glory—stood on the table brandishing a book in one hand and a spoon in the other, swinging it about as if it were a saber and the chandelier a swooping dragon to be vanquished. A voracious roar ripped out of him, rattling the dishes on the table under his feet. His shirt was untucked, but at least he wore one. The two youngest, Rory and little Birdie, who were still in their nightgowns with jam smeared from collar to hem, sat on the floor with an open jar of strawberry preserves.

"Children!" Belle clapped her hands sharply just as Mrs. Bakewell, the cook, careened into the room from a side door carrying a large ironstone pitcher.

The twins raced to Belle, wrapping their arms around the wet coat she had yet to remove. "Save us from Jack, Miss Beaumont!"

Forcing a stiff upper lip, she peeled Tibby and Pippin from her legs. "There will be no more running inside, so there's nothing to fret about. Jack! Cease your cavorting at once, or there will be no pudding for you after dinner tonight."

"Yes, Miss Beaumont." While his words agreed, the sloppy drop of his body into a chair said anything but.

She reached for Cricket, snagging the boy around the waist and pulling him from the table. "Nor will there be any more standing on the furniture. You all know better than this. What is the meaning of such bad behaviour?"

"No Graybills, that's what." Mrs. Bakewell swiped up one of the children's cups and sloshed water into it, the cap on her head askew. "And no milk either."

"I don't understand." She settled Cricket into a chair, then swooped over to the youngest pair, who were starting to paint their hair with the jam. "The solicitor said he'd spoken with them, and he's only just left. I should like to know the details of the fire in the main hall, and, by the by, why is there no milk for the children?"

"I can tell ye all that, Miss Beaumont," ten-year-old Anne

chimed in. "The Graybills said the nice man was to mind us until you came, though I dunno if he knew that. The fire just popped right out of the chimney last night, but I weren't a milksop about it. And now Jack is saying he's king over us all."

"Did not," Jack singsonged.

"Did too!" Anne shouted.

Jack shook his head. "Can't prove it."

Anne stuck out her tongue. "Nyah!"

Little Birdie started crying at the quarrel. Belle plucked the toddler from the floor—then instantly regretted the decision as the child wrapped her sticky arms around her neck, smearing jam on the bodice of her coat.

"Jack and Anne," Belle huffed. "As the oldest, I expect better manners than—"

The front door bell rang, shrilly interrupting her.

So did Mrs. Bakewell. "About that milkman, something needs to be done, and furthermore—"

"Excuse me, Mrs. Bakewell." Belle set Birdie down, untwining herself from the child's strong grip. "I will help you with the milkman debacle in a minute, and I should like a full accounting about that fire as well. For now, however, the door must be answered."

With clipped steps, she retraced her route to the front of the house, feet of varying strides pattering behind her. The moment she opened the door wide, a mountain of turnips careened toward her.

In came the Graybills, Joe pushing a rusty red wheelbarrow heaped with root vegetables. Betty carried the overflow in two buckets, dripping water and mud all over the floor.

Belle blinked, so stunned her voice barely squeaked. "What is this?"

Joe flashed a yellow-toothed grin. "Why, it's turnips for everyone, miss. The children will love them."

The cook swiped one off the top of the pile, lips curling into a sneer as she held it up. "More like turnips for all the swayback nags down at Boggins's Stable."

"I'll have you know, Mrs. Bakewell, that my Joe here"—Betty jutted her sharp chin toward her husband—"cut a wig-waggon o' a deal with old lady Nettle down at the market. Snagged 'em for free, he did, and it was either pick them up this morning or miss out on such a bounty."

"Bounty, my foot!" Mrs. Bakewell tossed the turnip back into the wheelbarrow. "Those ain't fit fer mashin' or boilin'. I can't feed these to the children."

"Good for juggling, though." Jack snatched three of them from Betty's bucket and set about circling the vegetables in the air.

A headache started to throb in Belle's temple. "Put those down, Jack."

Add to list: Hire a proper housekeeper. And possibly a lion tamer.

Mrs. Bakewell stamped her foot, swishing the blue-and-white-striped fabric of her sturdy skirts. "About that milk—"

"Make way!" Joe shouted. "I'll just wheel this lot down to the kitchen and—"

"Ow!" Pippin screamed and shoved his arm up toward Belle. "Rory bit me right here."

Rory ran in circles. Jack flung turnips in the air. Little Birdie had dragged the jam jar out to the hall and was rubbing her gooey fingers along the runner's hem, laughing uproariously. And all the while rain blew in through the open front door, where Cricket stamped his feet in the small pools collecting just beyond the threshold.

Belle pressed her fingers to her brow, pushing back the throbbing. How had Mrs. Trumble managed such chaos? Oh, how she wished the woman were here right now!

"Excuse me, but might I have a word with Mrs. Trumble?" A deep voice, one that could sway a jury with its magnificent timbre, pulled her gaze from Cricket to a tall man in a black hat standing just inside Haven House.

And the man was just as magnificent as his voice. Dark hair curled above his collar, luxurious in its thickness. Eyes the colour of a storm on an August horizon stared at her, a lift to one of his brows. He had a kindly face, one a girl might sneak peeks at from across a room. Wealth and power hung on his shoulders as tangibly as his finely tailored greatcoat. Belle immediately bristled, both from his obvious affluence and the sudden tingle traveling from her heart to her toes.

She lifted her chin, annoyed to be caught in such an obvious state of pandemonium. "Mrs. Trumble is . . . no longer here, sir. May I help you? I am—oh!" She toppled sideways as the twins crashed into her, Jack on their heels, wielding a turnip.

The man reached for her, his firm grip restoring her world—and his grin tearing it right down again, so dizzying was its brilliance. "It appears, madam, you are the one who could use some help."

Four

> They were not forty children conducting themselves like one, but every child was conducting itself like forty.
>
> —Charles Dickens, *A Christmas Carol*

In the midst of dripping turnips, shrieking children, stamping feet, and all-out anarchy, Rafe held an angel in his arms. Eyes the colour of rich Brazilian coffee blinked up into his. The woman's hair was the same mocha hue, with soft tendrils having escaped the pins, curled by rain. She smelled of ginger and cinnamon. Ahhh, of course. Angels ought to smell of Christmas.

"Are you all right?" He clamped his mouth shut the moment the question passed his lips. How ridiculous. She'd only lost her footing momentarily, not taken a dive off the side of a rampart.

"I am now, thank you." She pulled from his touch.

A loss, that. He clenched his hands to keep from reaching for her again, then promptly scolded himself for such lecherous behaviour. What the deuce had gotten into him?

"Excuse me for one moment, sir." She turned back to the ruckus, raising her voice above the melee. "Betty and Joe, please see that the children are properly dressed and taken to the playroom. There will be no school today. Mrs. Bakewell, you may clear the dining room and move on to luncheon preparations.

Jack, put those turnips down and help with the younger ones. You too, Anne. I shall meet with you all shortly."

The scarecrow of a man grasping the wheelbarrow handles gave a sharp nod toward the heap of misshapen vegetables. "What about the turnips, miss?"

A steel-haired matron with a swipe of flour along her cheek planted her fists on her hips. "And what about the milkman?"

"What about Jack prancin' about as king over us all?" cried a pug-nosed girl in braids.

One child, a carrot-topped lad of eight—maybe—elbowed a girl with flaming curls. "Race you to the playroom!"

"Hold it right there, young man." The woman he'd held only moments ago snagged the boy by the collar. "You know there's no running, and furthermore—"

She continued scolding, yet Rafe no longer heard, not when his gaze landed on a boy busily squishing his fingers into the dampened rug near the front door. He was an average little fellow, certainly not one to stand out in a crowd of children. Even so, a charge ran along Rafe's veins from head to toe. That upturned nose, the wavy brown hair that might be his very own, the same tilt to the lad's head that his sister always affected when sketching . . . the small dimple on the right side of the boy's mouth as he pressed his lips together, matching Jenny's. Rafe's heart squeezed.

Was this his sister's child?

A howl ripped out of the youngest children, pulling him from his study of the boy. What bedlam! This place needed the strong hand of a man who could bring order, which he could, had he the time.

Which he didn't.

Still, he'd not find out anything about the boy squishing his fingers into the waterlogged carpet unless something was done.

"There will be order in this household!" he bellowed with his courtroom tone.

Eleven pairs of eyes swung his way, the sudden silence a blessed gift.

"Good," he continued. "Now then, I believe the lady has made your orders clear enough, so step lively *and* quietly. Dismissed."

They filed off without a sound—save for the creak of the wheelbarrow heavy on the floorboards. A smirk twisted Rafe's lips. That had been surprisingly easy.

Yet that smirk vanished the moment the woman turned to him with fire in her eyes. "It is not your place, sir, to dismiss my staff or the children. Who are you, and what is your business at Haven House?"

It took all his effort not to raise his brows. What an anomaly. Many a clerk shrank in his presence, yet here this slip of a woman stood with a lift to her chin and censure in her tone. Surprisingly, he couldn't help but admire the affront.

"I beg your pardon. You are entirely correct. I am Rafe Munro, looking for a particular child who may be in residence here. And you are?"

"I am Miss Isabelle Beaumont, director and owner of this establishment . . . leastwise I shall be once the probate application is made and Mrs. Trumble's will is read."

He frowned. "Am I to understand Mrs. Trumble is deceased?"

"Yes."

"Hmm." He rubbed his chin, mind reeling at the news. His mother must not have heard the ill tidings yet. "May I ask how it happened?"

True sorrow etched the woman's brow. "There was a carriage accident Saturday evening in which Mrs. Trumble was thrown from the coach. She succumbed to the injuries a few hours later."

"That is quite unfortunate."

"Indeed, it is." She unbuttoned her coat, and as she pulled it off, only then did he realize she'd been wearing outdoor attire. She folded it over her arm while casting him a glance. "You spoke of a child. Who is it you are hoping to find?"

"My nephew or perhaps my niece. I am not entirely certain, but by my estimation, he or she would be five years of age."

"We do have a lad who is five."

"The one who was playing in the water just there?" He pointed at the darkened circle on the rug near the door.

"Yes." She nodded. "That is Cricket."

"Cricket?" This time his brows did shoot skyward. "The lad's namesake is an insect?"

Miss Beaumont's lips curved into a most becoming smile. "I can think of worse things to be known by. A cricket is a rather noble creature, sharing its music with one and all. Some even think them good luck."

"And others would as soon grind them beneath their heel." He mimicked her grin. "At any rate, I should like to see the paperwork on this Cricket."

"I'm afraid that is not possible, Mr. Munro. All orphanage files are confidential."

"Even to family members?"

"No, but you said yourself you do not know for certain if Cricket is the child you seek."

Ah, a quick mind and a quicker tongue. The woman would make a fine prosecutor were she a man. He met her even gaze. "I could know with a glance at the boy's pertinent information if you would simply allow it. I assure you I am not some nefarious kidnapper."

"I didn't mean to imply such." Her cheeks pinked, an adorable sight that was quite at odds with the stern set of her mouth. "Still, I would need more credentials from you other than your word and suspicions."

As much as he'd like to banter away the morning with this beauty, he needed to get to the office. Though it was egregiously opportunistic, he had no choice but to use his judicial expertise. "Miss Beaumont, I understand the importance of confidentiality in such matters. However, as a barrister, I am keenly aware that the law affords certain allowances, particularly when close relations make an inquiry as to the welfare of a child. In such cases, guardians and institutions are often compelled to provide information that might otherwise be kept private."

"I am not familiar with any such allowance." Uncertainty

wrinkled her brow. "But I can assure you Cricket's welfare is indisputably excellent. Haven House is exactly that—a loving refuge for those who have no family . . . despite a rather unfortunate chimney fire." She tipped her head toward the main hall.

"I do not question the boy's care, for despite the pandemonium I witnessed and the rather subpar state of your main hall, I trust that you are the sort who would do all in your power to see the children are well maintained. Still, this boy's lineage *is* in question, and because his welfare could significantly benefit from the knowledge of his true family, a cursory glance at the documents to confirm or refute my claim would be legally justifiable. And might I add, to withhold this information could possibly be construed as obstructing a legal inquiry, which I am certain you would wish to avoid."

She hugged her coat to her chest, jaw jutting. "Is that a threat, Mr. Munro?"

He stifled a wince. That's exactly what it was, yet this was no courtroom, and she was no defender to be cowed into submission. He softened his tone. "I do not mean to intimidate. Merely to state facts, Miss Beaumont."

"You are a very determined man, sir."

"I haven't the time to be anything other."

"I see." She loosened her grip on her coat and absently smoothed away the wrinkles. "Well, you will find me every bit as determined. I cannot—*will* not—show you those records unless you provide me with a legal document to do so."

Irritation mixed with his admiration for this bulwark in a gown. "Miss Beaumont, if you would—"

"But"—she held up a finger—"in order to preserve the integrity of our records and supply you with a satisfactory answer, I shall be more than happy to glance at Cricket's file myself to see if the name Munro is mentioned. Follow me."

She turned before he could answer, which was just as well. That way she didn't witness the drop of his jaw. The woman was as changeable as a spring wind, and he wasn't quite sure how to feel about being put so off balance.

He strode after her, catching up to Miss Beaumont as she hung her coat on a hook in an office that instantly set his teeth on edge. Files of documents sat in untidy heaps on the desktop, accompanied by assorted quills and inkstands in varying stages of usage. Atop file cabinets, papers hung out of bins. Brown parcel paper was folded sloppily into a stack in one corner, and in another was a leaning tower of books that would be better served lined up like soldiers on a shelf. The disarray of the place chafed like a wet woolen shirt.

"Have a seat, Mr. Munro." She pointed toward one of the two chairs in front of the massive desk. "This shouldn't take long."

Hopefully it wouldn't. Though as she pulled out one file drawer after another, he got the sinking feeling he might be here a very long time indeed.

"No," she murmured.

So then, the boy wasn't Jenny's after all. He rose, surprised at the disappointment clenching his gut. "I assume you have found my claim is moot, and so I thank you for your time, Miss Beaumont."

"No, that's just it." She glanced at him over her shoulder. "This drawer is supposed to contain the children's records. Leastwise I thought it was. If you wouldn't mind waiting a moment longer."

He did mind. Very much. Yet he sat once again as she moved on to another file cabinet, his gaze landing on the disorderly folders atop the desk. "You might try the files over here. Perhaps Mrs. Trumble was in the midst of some sort of housekeeping."

"I wish that were the case." Miss Beaumont turned to him with a stack of papers in her hand. "These are receipts for coal deliveries from five years ago. And these—" She exchanged the slips in her fingers for another bundle of notes. "Well, these are a very fine collection of Christmas pudding recipes."

He rubbed the back of his neck, muscles tightening at the complete confusion of Haven House's office. "Is there no order to the filing system?"

"Perhaps, but not one I can understand." She tucked the

papers away and shut the drawer. "Mrs. Trumble must have had her own methodology."

"Surely the children's records must be here somewhere."

"No doubt they are, but it will take days—possibly weeks—to sort through this madness." She sank into the big leather chair behind the desk. "I am sorry, Mr. Munro. You will have to come back at a later time. I had no idea things were in such a state. I have been a teacher here these past seven years, not an administrator. I'm afraid I am in a bit over my head." She waved her hand at the mess around her.

Clearly she was, and though a strange instinct to help her welled, he shoved it down. "A word of advice, Miss Beaumont. You ought to get some help. A secretary. A new teacher. A daytime nursemaid and some workmen to repair that front room."

"While I appreciate your counsel, sir, I—"

"Miss Beaumont?" A small voice entered the door at his back.

"Yes, Cricket?"

At the mention of the boy's name, Rafe turned and was once again struck by the uncanny resemblance this young lad bore to Jenny.

The boy wiggled one stockinged foot in the air. "I can't find my other shoe."

"You were in the playroom, were you not?" Miss Beaumont questioned. "Did you ask Mr. or Mrs. Graybill to help you find it?"

"Can't." He shook his head. "They're not there."

Miss Beaumont's brow creased. "Don't tell me Jack is king of the playroom."

"No, Mrs. Bakewell is in there."

"But she is supposed to be preparing lunch."

Cricket shrugged, his shoulders little knobs beneath his shirt.

Miss Beaumont stood. "I am sorry, Mr. Munro. Duty calls. Do you mind seeing yourself out?"

The lad pattered over to him and tugged on Rafe's trouser leg, his grey-blue eyes as large as coat buttons. "Have you seen my shoe, sir?"

Rafe's chest squeezed at the sight of the boy who was trying to manage on his own amidst the havoc. The innocence in Cricket's voice and the sight of his single shoe pulled at something deep inside him. He dropped to his knee, eye level with the lad. "I have not seen it, young master, but I am certain it must be in the playroom, for when you left the front hall, you had both shoes on your feet. Let's see, when I was a lad, I remember once leaving my shoe beneath a toy drum, and another time I set one on a windowsill. Can you think of an odd corner where you might have deposited your own shoe?"

Cricket's brows furrowed into a straight line, then just as suddenly, his eyes lit up. "You're right, sir! I might've. Thank you." He bolted out of the room.

"Oh, that boy," Miss Beaumont muttered fondly.

That boy, indeed. Rafe's heart softened toward the shoeless lad. Cricket needed a guardian. Miss Beaumont needed . . . well, she needed a whole host of help, truth be told. He could solve neither of those problems, and yet a certain amount of protectiveness for them both rose to the surface of his heart.

Which was entirely out of character for him when he ought to be focused on the Grindlethorn murder case.

He pulled out his watch and, after a quick glance, tucked the timepiece back into his pocket. He couldn't afford to dally here any longer today—but that didn't rule out tomorrow. With some finagling, and perhaps a bit less sleep, he could manage to eke out a modicum of spare minutes. For if his gut feeling that Cricket was Jenny's son was correct, he could do no less.

He rose. "I must be off, Miss Beaumont. However, I shall return tomorrow."

She angled her head. "I will not have sorted through any paperwork by then."

"Exactly, which is why you need my help."

She tossed back her shoulders, and while she kept her tone even, there was no denying she bristled. "I am quite capable of managing the affairs of Haven House."

"I'm sure you are, and yet circumstance suggests otherwise

for the moment. I am intimately acquainted with paperwork and will carve out an hour each morning to help you sort through this mess." With a sweep of his hand, he indicated the various heaps and piles. "Also, as fate would have it, I know of an organization that could coordinate your day-to-day operations. I will plead the case of Haven House this very night to the chairperson."

"I appreciate your accommodation, Mr. Munro." She pushed back her chair and stood, studying him with those endlessly brown eyes of hers. "But what if Cricket is not the child you seek? This could be a colossal waste of your time. And before we go any further, you must understand I'll need to review any sensitive documents myself. That is my one condition."

She was right on both accounts. This was no doubt a bad idea, especially in light of the serious case he must manage and that she ought to keep confidentiality at a premium.

But the niggling in his spirit grabbed hold of his common sense and gave it a good shake. "Agreed, Miss Beaumont." He gave her a sharp nod. "And with that, I bid you good day."

He strode down the corridor, her "Good day, Mr. Munro" following after him.

Collecting his umbrella by the front door, he stepped into the rain. Carving out an hour a day would be a feat in itself. Convincing his mother to resume her post as chair of the Society for Bettering the Condition and Increasing the Comforts of the Poor? That bordered on impossible.

But without the society's support, Miss Beaumont didn't stand a chance.

FIVE

> As to *her*, she was worthy to be his partner in every sense of the term. If that's not high praise, tell me higher, and I'll use it.
>
> —Charles Dickens, *A Christmas Carol*

Dawn was barely a whisper when Rafe threw off his counterpane and sprang from the bed, glad to be done with a fitful night of sleep that never quite came. The Grindlethorn murder case weighed heavily on his mind. He and Harvey had to prove the accused—Ward Davis—was innocent, and Rafe knew in his gut the young man was blameless. If it weren't for the nearsighted witness, Mrs. Hammer, who claimed she saw him fleeing the scene, it would be an open-and-shut matter. Today he'd poke about the Marylebone neighbourhood and inquire if anyone else had seen anything.

After he stopped by Haven House . . . which was another reason he hadn't slept well. He shrugged into a fresh shirt, then swiped a grey silk waistcoat from the wardrobe. The few times he had drifted off last evening, all he could see was Cricket's face superimposed over Jenny's. Not definitive proof, and yet he would be surprised to discover the boy wasn't her son. That is, *if* he could discover anything at all in that rat's nest of an office.

Grabbing his frock coat, he strode out the door, shoving his arms into the sleeves as he trotted downstairs. Scaffolding yet filled the front hall, but at least there'd been some progress yesterday.

He swung into the dining room, intending to drink a cup of tea and be gone, yet there sat his mother, tapping a butter knife at the shell of a soft-boiled egg. He glanced at her from the sideboard. "You're up early. Then again, you retired early last night. I had hoped to have a word with you when I got home from the office."

"A megrim came on late in the afternoon, so I took to my room."

He frowned while reaching for the teapot. "I am sorry to hear it. I hope you are quite recovered."

"I am, thank you." She peeled off the top of her egg, then dug in with her spoon. "What were you wanting to talk with me about?"

"I stopped by Haven House yesterday." He sank into an adjacent chair. "Did you know Mrs. Trumble is recently deceased?"

"Oh . . . my." She set down her spoon, drawing in a shaky breath. "I had no idea. I hope she didn't suffer, poor dear."

He shook his head. "From my understanding it was an accident, and she didn't linger overlong."

"Thank God for such a mercy."

Steam rose from his cup, and he blew it off before taking a sip. "But she is already sorely missed at the orphanage. The place was in quite a shambles, the new director being young and inexperienced. She could do with help from your society, Mother. Immediate help. Might you contact the committee members and call a meeting posthaste on behalf of your old friend Mrs. Trumble?"

"I could, but . . ." Her lips pinched into a clamshell, a favorite thinking posture of hers. At length, she once again picked up her spoon. "Is it truly a need, or is this your way of surreptitiously getting me out of the house?"

"It is no secret I wish you would venture out, but I am not fabricating the dire situation of the place. Miss Beaumont will need guidance in restoring the burned-out main hall—which was an unfortunate mishap with a chimney that I suspect ought to have been swept more thoroughly. She will also require help in hiring staff to manage the children. I myself have pledged to help with the tangled web of paperwork for an hour each morning before I go to the office. In fact, I really ought to run right now." He slung back the tea, which promptly burned a hot line from his tongue to his belly.

Mother narrowed her eyes. "Why did you go to Haven House yesterday?"

Now, there was an indicting question. How did he blithely say he was seeking an out-of-wedlock child that might be her own flesh and blood? Though he had his suspicions about Cricket, he didn't know for certain the lad was Jenny's. It wouldn't do to get his mother's hopes up only to dash them on the rocks. He set his cup on the saucer, carefully choosing his words. "With our talk of Jenny the other day, I thought I'd see the place firsthand. Call it nostalgia, if you will."

"The great barrister of Lincoln's Inn feeling sentimental?" She dabbed her lips with her serviette, eyeing him with a scrutiny many a judge would love to perfect. "I thought the case you were on was all-consuming."

"It is, which is why I'm only helping Miss Beaumont minimally."

"Hmm." She set the white linen square on the table, then pushed away her half-eaten egg. "Tell me about this new director."

And there was the other reason he'd not slept last night. Though he'd only been in Miss Beaumont's presence for a scant half hour, she'd left an indelible mark. For the life of him, he couldn't think why. Perhaps because she'd stood up to him so fearlessly? Or was it her unique scent of Christmas and enigmatic stare that stuck with him?

But he couldn't very well tell his mother that.

He shifted uncomfortably in his chair. "Apparently, Miss Beaumont has been a teacher there the past seven years. I would imagine she knew Jenny, though I haven't inquired as of yet. She is . . . feisty, to say the least, which will serve her well in her new position. I can see why Mrs. Trumble bequeathed Haven House to her, for once she gets her footing, I believe she'll be a force to be reckoned with as a stalwart advocate for the children."

"Is that so?" his mother murmured. "What colour were her eyes?"

"A deep, rich brown," he answered without effort, then cocked his head. "Why do you ask?"

"Why did you notice?"

"I am a barrister"—he shrugged—"amply compensated for paying attention to detail."

"Mm-hmm." A knowing smile curved his mother's mouth. "And what colour are Miss Greenbrough's eyes?"

"What a ridiculous question. I fail to see what Miss Greenbrough has to do with this discussion."

"You grew up with her. You see her at every social function. She dotes on you exclusively." Mother leaned toward him. "So again, I ask, what colour are her eyes?"

"This is absurd. They are . . ." Great heavens. Were they blue? Brown? Green? Who knew? Certainly not him.

Ah. So that was what this little game was about. Mother would no doubt have him proposing to Miss Beaumont before nightfall merely because he'd recalled a simple facial feature.

He pushed back his chair more forcefully than necessary. "I'm going to be late. Do pull that committee together and see what resources can be given to Haven House. Until tonight, Mother." He brushed a light kiss to the top of her head, then stalked to the door.

"Oh, Rafe?"

He paused on the threshold.

"The Christmas Open House invitations arrived yesterday and are in the drawing room. Why don't you bring one to your Miss Beaumont?"

He rolled his eyes. "She is not mine, Mother."

A sly twinkle gleamed in her gaze. "Not yet."

Belle awoke with a start, trying to make sense of her strange surroundings and even stranger dream about a handsome man with stormy blue eyes and a smile that warmed her from the inside out. Her gaze slowly focused on the open file drawers and desk stacked with folders. The office. She'd stayed up late sorting through the paperwork Mr. Munro had so graciously offered to help her with. Both the man and the mess must have been on her mind when she had fallen asleep hunched over the desk.

Rising, she cracked her neck one way, then the other, as she crossed to the only window. Dawn barely eased the gloom of another cloudy day. The boxwood hedge was nothing but a dark line, separating the orphanage from the plot of land where the Radcliffe House had once stood. Nothing of that building remained except some crumbling foundation stones. Belle frowned. The scene would be much cheerier with a light coating of snow.

And yet the sky still refused to cooperate with any sort of Christmas spirit.

Add to list: Cut paper snowflakes with the children and hang from ceiling. Sleep in bed tonight instead of draped over a piece of furniture.

Her gaze drifted back to the desk. How many mornings had Mrs. Trumble sat right there, running Haven House with an unshakable will? An ache carved a hollow in Belle's chest. Oh, how she missed the woman!

But no time to fret about such things. The children would soon stir, and she'd best be ready to face another busy day. First order of business, a splash of cold water to her face and a fresh gown.

She set off at a brisk pace toward the front staircase and had just gained the first step when a light knock rapped on the door. She froze, debating what to do, for surely it was Mr. Munro. He'd said he'd come early, but *this* early? She couldn't very well greet the man in the abysmally wrinkled gown she'd worn yesterday, her hair a frightful mess and eyes puffy from so little sleep. Nor could she dash upstairs to rouse the Graybills to answer the door for fear of also waking the children.

Yet neither could she ignore the knocking, for Mr. Munro was clearly a gent used to getting his own way.

Three more raps.

Bother!

Shoving down a wave of mortification, she tucked loose waves into what remained of her chignon. Mr. Munro, in all his wealth and glory, would no doubt look down his nose at her rumpled appearance. Ben would have.

La! Would she never be free of that man's judgment? Ten years had passed since that horrible scene when she'd accused him of displacing her in his heart with an idol—a golden one. Greed. She'd meant it, every word—still did—but she could also yet see the coldness in his eyes, the way he'd let her go without a fight. How he'd weighed and measured her against his ambitions.

And found her lacking.

Pushing away the horrid memory, she reached for the doorknob.

Then blinked. "Father?"

"So you do remember who I am, though to be fair, it's only been a day since I last saw you." He winked. "I thought I'd stop by to give you a proper good-bye."

"Good-bye? Where are you going? Oh, do come in." She ushered him into the front hall—and that's when it hit her. With the main room still in shambles, there was no good place to receive a visitor . . . just one more problem to be added to her overwhelming must-do list.

"Egads!" Her father stared at the damage in the main room. "What happened here?"

"A chimney fire, unfortunately, though thank God it was contained, and no one was hurt. It will take some doing, but I am determined to have the area restored before Christmas."

"And heaven help anyone who stands in your way." He chuckled, then sobered. "But this is too much for you to manage. Not alone. I am to set off by coach for a week of business meetings in Liverpool, but I will reschedule until January. I shall stay here and help you instead."

How like him to make such an offer, and yet if she would be a director, she must learn to do things on her own. She smoothed the lapels of his greatcoat, love swelling for a father who cared so much he'd put his own schedule on hold. "No, there is no need."

"Did I not tell you to accept help when it is offered?"

"I don't need any help, truly."

"My sweet Belle." He gathered her hands. "Let me assist you."

"But, Father, I—"

Another round of knocking echoed in the hall. She pulled from her father's touch with a small smile. "Excuse me a moment."

She opened the door to an immaculately dressed Mr. Munro, cutting quite a striking figure against the grey of an early morn. Every detail of his attire reflected his wealth and status, from the tip of his tailored greatcoat to the hem of his slim-fitting trousers. His direct blue gaze—almost roguish with that silver gleam—assessed her from beneath the brim of a black silk hat. The flash in his eyes wasn't condemning so much as perplexed. And for good reason. How often did a woman of position answer her own door, and in a rumpled gown, no less?

Add to list: Hire a maid-of-all-work. Find hairbrush or borrow a mobcap.

"Good morning, Miss Beaumont. I hope you were expecting me?"

"Yes, of course, Mr. Munro." Swallowing her embarrassment, she stepped aside. "Do come in."

The calming scent of bay rum aftershave traveled with him as he passed her. She closed the door, then turned to find her father and Mr. Munro exchanging glances. But of course they were. It was odd enough to have one man in the front hall at so early an hour, let alone two.

She quickly stepped between them. "Father, this is Mr. Rafe Munro, a barrister who has offered to help me sort out the rather dismal state of affairs Mrs. Trumble left behind in the office. And, Mr. Munro, I should like to introduce my father, Mr. Charles Beaumont."

"Pleased to meet you, sir." Mr. Munro doffed his hat while giving a slight bow.

Her father smiled. "The pleasure is mine, Mr. Munro. Your reputation precedes you, for I have heard nothing but good in connection with your name. I had not realized Mrs. Trumble maintained such esteemed connections within the legal fraternity."

"Actually, I never met the woman."

"And yet here you are."

"Indeed." Mr. Munro flashed a smile of his own. "And so you find me."

Her father's gaze bounced between her and the dapper Mr. Munro, a sly twist growing on his lips the longer he stared. "I see," he murmured, then louder, "Well, far be it from me to keep the two of you from diving into that paperwork. I have a coach to catch. Good-bye, my dear." He embraced her, a quiet whisper warming her ear before he pulled away. "I see my worries about you meeting a potential husband were in vain."

Instant heat rushed to her cheeks. "You are incorrigible," she said under her breath.

He grinned wide as he turned to Mr. Munro. "Good day, sir."

"Good day, Mr. Beaumont." He dipped his head.

"Good-bye, Father." Once again Belle closed the door, then faced Mr. Munro. "I hope you don't mind waiting here a few moments while I freshen up. I won't be long."

"You need not do so on my account." His fine, wide lips curved on one side, a dimple appearing on his cheek. "You look lovely as you are."

Oh dear. Surely he was used to women fawning over him. Was that what he thought she was doing? She squared her shoulders, determined to look anything but coquettish. "It is kind of you to say so, sir, but I wasn't fishing for praise."

"Nor did I take it as such. My words are a statement of fact, not an idle compliment. In my profession, empty words hold no worth."

Warmth flashed through her again, and she was surprisingly—much to her chagrin—unsure how to reply.

"I am curious, though," he continued, "as to why you are wearing the same gown as yesterday. Is everything all right with the children? I hope you weren't kept up nursing one of them."

She pressed her palms to her belly, forcing her hands to keep from smoothing out wrinkles. What was the point? He'd already noticed. "Thank you for your concern, but the children are all fine. I merely wished to make some progress in the office before you arrived this morning."

His brows shot to the rafters. "Do not tell me you stayed up all night because of me."

"No, I mean, yes, I—em . . ." She flattened her lips. How could one man so twaddle up her words that she sounded like a schoolgirl stumbling over her mathematic recitations?

Really, Isabelle! Pull yourself together. He's only a man, not a headmaster come to rap your knuckles.

Lifting her chin, she forced her gaze to meet his. "Suffice it to say I was not awake the entire evening, as evidenced by the creases in my gown."

"Mmm," he rumbled, turning his hat about in his hands. "Sorting out paperwork is not worth your health, Miss Beaumont. I fear you are overdoing it—and this is only your second day as director."

"Any worthwhile venture takes effort at the onset. My father owes his rise to wealth to such a dictum. I can do no less. Haven House deserves such dedication."

She drew strength from that sentiment, confident that by following her father's example she would be no less successful. Growing up in a lower-middle-class family had its challenges, but by her father's industry and God's good grace, he'd been able to establish a booming shipping business, elevating them in society. Not to the standards of the handsome man in front of her, mind, but nonetheless to a respectable station.

Mr. Munro set his hat on the coat-tree and unbuttoned his greatcoat, casting her a glance. "I admire your devotion to industry and orphans, yet I insist you spend no more evenings sleeping at your desk. If you find my services are not enough, then I shall happily recommend a clerk to take on the more menial tasks of ledgers and records."

She inhaled sharply. "I did not mean to imply your work here would be lacking. La, sir! You have such a way of tangling my tongue."

"It's a habit, I suppose." He grinned as he shrugged out of his coat. "Works well in the courtroom, but in real life, I admit it can be a downfall. Go, then. I shall wait here on this sturdy little couch." He sidestepped to a bench. The wood creaked as he sank, and one of the legs angled precariously crooked.

She winced.

Add to list: Fix hall bench. And retrieve spoon currently propping up the back leg.

"Thank you, Mr. Munro. I won't be long." She turned toward the stairs.

"Oh, before I forget, take this with you."

Retracing her steps, she retrieved the white envelope he held out. "What is this?"

"An invitation to a Christmas open house."

She offered it back. "Thank you very much, but I don't think I will have the time for such festivities. Surely you understand."

He folded his arms, a playful tilt to his head. "What I understand from the very short time I have known you, Miss Beaumont, is that you tend to overwork. As do I. Thus, such an event will likely be good for both of us."

A smile twitched her lips. If nothing else, the man was forthright, and despite her preconception that his wealth tainted his character, she couldn't help but admire him. "Do you really believe that, sir?"

"Not at all." He grinned. "But this party is a tradition neither of us can avoid. My mother's open house is more than a social diversion. Every committee member, benefactor, and would-be philanthropist in London attends. As my mother's son, I cannot avoid being there. And you . . . well, I suspect you'll be the newest darling of the season, which could benefit Haven House."

Amusement sparked in his eyes. "So I'll expect to see you there, Miss Beaumont."

Six

"No space of regret can make amends for one life's opportunity misused."

—Charles Dickens, *A Christmas Carol*

Five days of endurance was a modest sort of accomplishment, but one Belle wore as an invisible badge of honour. She'd withstood nearly a week here at Haven House. The orphanage had been a whirlwind of chaos with the children overly needy, a continual shuffle of repairmen arriving to give estimates, and posting notices for a teacher and a housekeeper. Each task completed seemed to breed three more, a relentless cycle of duties and demands. Yet despite her weariness, she remained resolute to bring order to the orphanage. For the briefest of moments, right there in the back garden with children running around the frozen fountain, she closed her eyes and relished the cold kiss of the afternoon breeze. Still no snow, but if the temperature continued to drop, perhaps soon the world would wear white.

A tug at her skirt drew her gaze to large grey-blue eyes staring up at her. Every time she looked at young Cricket, she thought of Mr. Munro. How hopeful he was to find the paperwork on this boy, and yet they'd still not uncovered the files. Deep down, she had a rogue desire they might never find them because she enjoyed the man's intelligence and humble humor. An hour a day with him only left her hungering for more. It was odd, this stirring in her heart, a sensation she hadn't felt since her younger years, when Ben had courted her . . . at least until money and power became his first love.

"Miss Beaumont," Cricket's high-pitched voice rose above Tibby and Pippin's squealing. "May we have tea and milk now?"

"Brilliant idea. I'm sure everyone would appreciate a warm-up." She turned to the children. "It is time for tea and biscuits in the dining room."

"Oh boy!" Jack whooped, practically knocking over Rory in his dash to the door.

Isabelle grabbed the three-year-old's hand, then collected little Birdie's as well. The rest of the children plowed after Jack, almost tripping Joe Graybill as he exited with a huge pickaxe hefted over his shoulder.

A pickaxe? What in the world?

Belle narrowed her eyes. "I thought you and Betty were seeing to the final cleanup in the main hall before the workmen arrive tomorrow morning."

He stopped in front of her, resting the sharp end of the tool on the gravel. "Betty has it under control. Leastwise I think she does. Though, come to think of it . . ." He scratched the stubble on his jaw. "Guess I haven't seen her in the past hour."

A sigh deflated her. Betty and Joe were the most agreeable of people but never seemed to carry out what they'd agreed to. "And the pickaxe? Surely you weren't trying to do repairs yourself?"

He laughed, his big nose honking on the inhales. "None of it, miss. Thought it was time for some iceberg removal."

Icebergs! Of all things. She shook her head with a tsk. "We are hardly in the middle of an ocean."

"I meant the fountain, miss. There's a chill in the air today. Can't have it freezing up and cracking."

"And yet by using a pickaxe you will accomplish the same dire end."

He blinked, mouth agape. "Oh. Right. Din't think o' that."

Rory yanked on her hand. "Biscuit! Biscuit!"

Little Birdie took up the chant as well.

"Patience, children." She gave them a stern look, then faced Joe. "I would prefer if you went back to removing the debris in the main hall. Then the workmen will have space to begin making their repairs tomorrow."

"Good idea, miss." He pivoted, the arc of the axe nearly whapping into her shins.

Add to list: confiscate all tools from Joe. Especially ones that are sharp.

Giving the man plenty of lead space, she guided the two youngest inside, then peeled off their coats to hang on hooks beside the door. She'd barely removed Birdie's hat before the two-year-old darted down the corridor to the dining room, shrieking all the way.

Isabelle pressed her lips together. Yelling at the child would only add to the noise. "Come along, Rory." Once again she grabbed the lad's hand and delivered him to the dining room, where a great game of chase circled the large table. This time she did raise her voice. "Children! Find your chairs. I shall ring for Mrs. Bakewell to bring your tea at once."

Frustrated, she yanked more forcefully than necessary on the velvet cord just as Betty swung into the room with an armful of mewling kittens. "Someone at the door for ye, miss."

"Kitties!" Chair legs scuffed the floor. One tipped over completely in the mad rush to crowd about Betty.

"I wanna hold one!" Pippin and Tibby jumped up and down.

Belle frowned. "What, pray tell, are you doing with those cats?"

"Bosh, miss! Why, they're for the children, o' course. Nothin' better than a furry friend at Christmastime." Bending, she handed out balls of fur. "Here ye be, Pippin. Share with yer sister. There's one for you, Anne. Cricket, why don't you take this one and play with Rory and little Birdie?"

"Hey!" Jack stepped up. "What about me?"

Belle grabbed bunches of her skirt to keep from snatching all the cats away, for it was too late now. The damage had been done.

Add to list: Ban all animals with whiskers until further notice.

"Betty," she grumbled under her breath. "We cannot care for three new creatures. Not now."

"Four, miss." The woman pulled out one more fluffy kitten. "Here ye be, Jack." She handed the cat to him, then turned to Belle. "And ye still have someone a-waitin' for ye in the hall, miss."

Of course she did—and whoever it was likely wasn't the bearer of good news. Calamity after calamity was the way of it and had been ever since she'd arrived last Monday.

Guilt nipped as she fled the cheerful commotion. The children were happy at least. Was that so bad? The Graybills always put the orphans first—though often ahead of common sense—and the children dearly loved them. In a world of uncertainty, Betty and Joe were a constant in their lives. A family, so to speak. Mrs. Trumble had understood that. So should she.

She upped her pace, determined to change her attitude. Who was to say her caller brought bad tidings? Inwardly she scolded herself. What kind of person assumed the worst at every turn? She knew better than to let pessimism take root. Hadn't she come to Haven House to bring hope to these children? If she couldn't muster hope for herself, how was she to manage to do so for the young lives under her care?

Giving herself a mental shake, she squared her shoulders and approached the front hall, where Mr. Snably stood peering at the fire damage. "Good afternoon, Mr. Snably."

He turned at her approach. "Ah, Miss Beaumont. I see things are still a bit, well . . ." His gaze drifted back to the ruined main hall. "Not quite put back together."

"It hasn't even been a week yet, Mr. Snably. These things take time." She swept her hand back toward the way she'd come. "Shall we retire to my office?"

"No need. I won't be long. I should think you'll have an

immediate answer for me after you read this." He retrieved an envelope from his coat pocket and held it out.

Curious, Belle removed a folded paper, and the more she read of the fine penmanship on the creamy page, the more her lips parted. Someone wished to purchase Haven House for an exorbitant sum. Immediately. She glanced up at Mr. Snably. "But . . . the orphanage is not on the market. Why would someone make an offer? And who is that someone?"

"I'm not sure who, exactly. The proposal was given me by a Mr. Smallbone, a solicitor working out of Cranberg Associates. He was in probate court when I filed the paperwork for Haven House. Apparently he mentioned the situation to one of his clients, who is interested in this property."

"In the property?" She angled her head. "But what about the orphans?"

"Yes, well, once you sell, there is no guaranteeing the building would be maintained as an orphanage."

Alarm prickled up her arms. "Mr. Snably, you specifically told me that as sole heir of Haven House it was up to me to manage the facility, or you would have had to make other arrangements. Surely those other arrangements you spoke of were not throwing the children out on the streets—and at Christmastime, no less!"

His head reared back. "That is quite harsh, Miss Beaumont. I meant no such thing."

And there she went again. Thinking the worst. What had come over her? Hah! That was an easy answer. Too much stress and too little sleep. Even so, the spidery man in front of her didn't deserve such vitriol.

She dipped her chin. "Pardon me, Mr. Snably. I've had little sleep of late, yet that is no excuse for being snappish. I pray you will forgive me."

"Oh, dear lady." He patted her arm gently. "I realize this has been a jarring experience for you. So think for a moment, if you will, how with an offer like this, you could place the children in other institutions that are larger and have more to offer. Then you could retire as a lady of leisure. And do not neglect to give a care to your father. What a burden would be lifted from his shoulders to know you would be amply provided for after his demise."

Her heart lurched at the thought of losing her father. Her grief for Mrs. Trumble—while all very real and heartrending—would be nothing in comparison. And yet Mr. Snably was right. If Father saw such a sum being offered, he would likely counsel her to take the money, especially considering the humble beginnings of their family. Why, she could even provide for him, and he could retire as well. And the children . . . A larger orphanage might have more benefits for them than this small home.

Bah! What was she thinking? This home was filled with love and merriment, as evidenced by the happy squeals drifting out from the dining room. Granted, there was too much laughter at times, but the children were happy. No one could put a price on that.

She refolded the letter. "I cannot help but wonder, Mr. Snably, what do you get out of the deal?"

"Me?" He sniffed as he straightened his lapels, gaze averted. "Ten percent," he murmured.

No wonder he was amenable to the idea.

"Mrs. Trumble entrusted these children, this house, to me. I cannot accept this offer." She handed back the letter. "Besides, I don't think I have the authority to do so anyway, being that the will has not yet been proved."

He clicked his tongue. "A mere technicality." Eyeing the paper, he hesitated before accepting it with a sad little shake to his head. "A proposal of this magnitude will not come your way again. I realize the novelty of the place is still fresh, as you've only been here five days, but even so, I beg you to reconsider. This is a life-altering sum."

"There is more to life than money, sir, and so I respectfully decline."

"Mmm, such is your prerogative. Still, I will hold on to this—

for a time—just in case you come to your senses and realize what a tremendous mistake you are making."

Retrieving his hat from the coat-tree, he clapped it on, his words echoing the sentiments of another man from her past. She remembered the day clearly when she'd broken off her engagement with Ben. She could still visibly recall the disbelief in his eyes when she'd told him she couldn't marry a man whose heart was so consumed by the pursuit of wealth. He'd insisted money was security, and without it there was no future. But she'd stood her ground, refusing to tie her life to someone who valued riches above all else.

And now, as she escorted Mr. Snably to the door, she felt the same pang of disappointment she'd felt with Ben. Was she destined to always encounter men who saw naught but the material value of things?

Her heart sank as she bade the solicitor good-bye, a foreboding thought lodging in her mind. She was drawn to Mr. Munro—undeniably so—but he was a wealthy man. Did he, too, prioritize money over all else? Until she knew for certain, she must be careful around him. Guard her thoughts, her emotions, and especially her heart.

For she refused to face the same heartbreak again.

Late Friday afternoons at the office were best spent drafting last-minute documents to be filed, conferring with partners on case intricacies, and signing endless pages of briefs, affidavits, and motions ad nauseam. Indeed, these things ought to be done. *Needed* to be done. Yet here Rafe sat, rolling a pen between his fingers, barely listening to Charles Harvey drone on as he paced in front of Rafe's desk. Rafe could barely hear the older barrister, for the enigmatic Miss Beaumont kept intruding upon his thoughts. How could a woman he'd met a mere five days ago take up so much space in his head?

He shifted in his seat, giving the appearance of rapt attention and, to be fair, tried to listen. Random words registered occasionally through the haze of the strange new feelings Miss Beaumont excited. He was attracted to her, all right. There was no denying it anymore. But it wasn't just her beauty that appealed to him, though admittedly those striking brown eyes of hers had captured his soul. No, it was more that she knew her mind, but not in an overbearing sort of fashion. He admired her unwavering dedication to the orphanage, her resolve to bring hope to a place that was currently an odd farrago of chaos and merriment. Her intelligence, her wit, the way she engaged him in conversations that were both challenging and enlightening . . . All those things combined into a woman who was truly extraordinary.

Not that he'd breathe a word of this to his mother. She'd have him wed by Sunday.

"—the summary?"

Harvey's question hung in the air like a thick fog.

"Sorry." Rafe set down the pen as he peered at the man. "What was that?"

Harvey stared at him with a piercing ice-blue gaze, a boon in the courtroom when cross-examining a witness but deucedly uncomfortable when that same stare skewered him now. Charles Harvey was a contradiction of a barrister, the hump on his nose a testament to a rebellious youth while the silver wisping through his hair lent him a distinguished air. His cheeks were ruddy, for he was an outdoorsman at heart, but the paunch of his belly spoke of far too much time spent in a leather chair. Whereas Rafe was driven by passion and a reckless desire for justice, Harvey's voice of reason was a good balance. God had known exactly what He was doing when early in his career at the bar Rafe had been housed in the same chambers with this man.

Harvey waved a document in the air. "I asked if you agreed with the changes I made to the summary statement."

Rafe masked a wince. He really should have been listening. "Why don't you reread it so I can be certain."

A snort whistled out of Harvey's nose, an unspoken indictment of Rafe's inattention, yet he lifted the page to within inches of his face and read once again. "Good gentlemen of the jury, on August seventh, Thomas Grindlethorn was believed murdered in his London home. The room bore signs of violence—a broken window, an overturned chair, a scorched hearth, and what authorities presume to be his remains, though the body was admittedly unidentifiable. A fireplace poker was found nearby, possibly a weapon, but the fire obscured much of the scene, making conclusions uncertain. Mrs. Hammer claims she saw my client, Ward Davis, fleeing the property, but her distance and poor eyesight cast real doubt. No one saw the act. No clear motive exists. And the evidence, what remains of it, is murky at best."

Harvey dropped into the chair, leather creaking. "Well? Did you hear me that time?"

"Loud and clear."

"And?" Harvey set the paper on the desk.

"Not bad for a draft. It needs some embellishment, however. I'll work on it tonight." Rafe tucked the document into a thick file, surprisingly not relishing a task he'd usually enjoy. Honestly, he'd rather be at Haven House tonight, working to prove Cricket was Jenny's son. He wanted the boy to be, for he'd grown fond of him. The lad had an uncanny way of seeking him out to help tie his shoe or show him a drawing he'd sketched astonishingly well for a child of his age. Cricket had a talent for illustrating, much like Jenny.

"Here, you'll need to sign this."

Rafe startled, surprised to find Harvey standing at his side, pointing a podgy finger at a sheet of paper laid in front of him. Rafe picked up his pen and dipped it in the inkstand, reminded of all the many papers he'd gone over this week with Miss Beaumont. Not a one of them had anything to do with Cricket or any of the other current residents of the orphanage. Bah! If only they could find where Mrs. Trumble had filed those documents.

He lowered the pen, only to have Harvey bat away his hand. "Munro! Where is your head, man?"

Rafe glanced at him, thoroughly confused and not just a little annoyed at the ink splotch pooled on his desk. He grabbed a blotting paper to clean the mess. "You said to sign that one."

"Yes, but not on that line!" Harvey replaced the page and tapped where Rafe had been about to pen his signature.

Rafe sucked in a breath. Blast! He'd nearly voided the whole thing. He redipped the pen and took extra care this time, signing with a flourish, then handed the paper to Harvey with a sheepish smile. "Thank you."

Harvey frowned. "This isn't like you. What is going on?"

"Nothing."

"Well," his friend said dryly, "that nothing better be resolved when our case goes to court in little over a fortnight. Mr. Davis is counting on us to win his freedom."

His shoulders sank beneath the weight of such a responsibility, but even so, he jutted his jaw. "We will win the case."

Harvey regarded him for a long moment. Only God knew what went on behind those clear blue eyes. "Look, Rafe, if you want me to take this one on solo, just say the word."

Rafe shook his head. "I appreciate the offer, but there is no need. I fully intend to pull my fair share of weight."

Skepticism twisted Harvey's mouth. "At least take off a day or two. I fear you are wearing yourself too thin."

Rafe grinned. "You sound like my mother."

"Intelligent woman. Just . . . think on it. A respite might do you good, freshen the mind, sharpen the wits. After all, we'll be going before Judge Flintwick."

He shook his head. "The Grindlethorn case is slated for Judge Ambersmyth."

"Didn't you hear?" Harvey's brows drew into a single line. "Ambersmyth had a riding injury on Wednesday. He'll be laid up until after Twelfth Night."

Rafe shoved down a growl. No, he most definitely had not heard. Judge Flintwick was notorious for siding with the prosecutor—*any* prosecutor.

It wouldn't matter a whit how solid of a defense he and Harvey presented.

SEVEN

"And therefore I am about to raise your salary!"
—Charles Dickens, *A Christmas Carol*

Mondays had never been a problem. Until a week ago, that is. Exhausted, Belle shoved back a loose curl and stared out the playroom window at the dismal afternoon. No snow yet. But no rain either. Just a cloak of grey fog blending the world into a blur . . . exactly like the past week. She'd entertained high hopes for her first seven days at Haven House, but all she'd managed was sorting through a single file cabinet—and that thanks only to Mr. Munro's help. She'd also ruined her best apron during the kittens-up-the-chimney debacle *and* stubbed her toe quite soundly when chasing a goose down the main hall after the Graybills attempted to barter laundry services with poultry.

A sigh leaked out of her. So much for crafting a wonderful Christmas for the children. She hadn't had one spare minute to devote to that yet. She hadn't even been able to resume her teaching responsibilities, something she must remedy soon, for the children needed a regular schedule.

Add to list: Lower expectations. And invest in sounder footwear.

She pressed her forehead to the frigid glass, trying hard to ignore that offer from Mr. Snably. It was such a tidy sum in exchange for walking away from what might be her biggest mistake. The children deserved better than she was currently managing. Was it cowardly to give up? Perhaps. But with each fresh mishap, the idea swelled ever larger.

Mrs. Trumble had believed she could do this. She'd trusted her—of all people—to carry on the work she had built. That trust now felt like a weight, one Belle wasn't sure she could shoulder. Oh, how she wished for an audible word of encouragement from that dear lady right now! But Mrs. Trumble's voice would never again fill these rooms, and that truth stung sharper than the cold glass against her brow.

Turning from the window, she glanced at the mantel clock. Nearly half past two. Rafe had promised to return this morning to help with the remaining records, but he hadn't appeared. Not even a note. Not like him. Leastwise, not the *him* she thought she'd come to know. And—though she'd never say it aloud—she admired. Maybe even slightly depended upon. A little. Unless it was just the chaos talking. Perhaps he was merely the nearest lifeline to grab.

"Miss Beaumont?" A small voice accompanied a tug at her skirt.

She glanced down to the wide blue-grey eyes of Cricket, standing there solemnly clutching a worn copy of *The History of Little Goody Two-Shoes* to his chest. Stooping nose to nose with the child, she brushed a stray swath of hair from his face. "What is it, young master?"

His mouth twisted. "Why, I'm no master, miss. Jack says I'm a no-account sprite what slipped in through the cracks and never left."

She pressed her lips tight, suppressing a frown. She'd have to have another talk with Jack about that hurtful tongue of his. "Well, I happen to have a special fondness for sprites. Now, what can I do for you?"

His toe made little circles on the rug, his head tilting shyly. "You said we could practice our carols."

Behind him, the twins, Tibby and Pippin, fought over a top,

and she wagged a finger at the bickering duo before smiling at him. "So I did—and so we shall."

Straightening, she was about to clap her hands to gather the children over to the piano when in through the door stumbled a mountain of paper-wrapped parcels.

"How about a little help?" Rafe's voice traveled from behind the stack of precariously balanced boxes in his arms.

"Oh boy!" Jack, being the tallest—and the one with the longest legs—reached him first, swiping at several packages.

Which only caused the rest to tumble.

Children swarmed around the bounty, laughing, chattering, and tearing at the paper.

And thoroughly horrifying Belle with their savage manners.

"Children!" She rapped her knuckles on the top of the old wooden piano. "There will be no treacle tart after dinner if you continue this beastly behaviour."

Eyes turned her way, fingers now dead still on whatever present they held. All save for two-year-old Birdie, who could only ever think about what was right in front of her at any given moment.

Mr. Munro chuckled as he strode to Belle. "It's Saint Nicholas Day. Let them celebrate."

"Please, Miss Beaumont? May we open the gifts Mr. Munro brought?" Anne dipped her chin, batting her eyelashes like a professional actress.

"Pwease?" Rory echoed, his appeal shooting straight to Belle's heart.

How was she to refuse that?

If she was going to give in, though, it would not serve to appear so easily swayed. She folded her hands in front of her, shoulders militarily stiffened. "You may open your gifts only after you thank Mr. Munro for his thoughtfulness."

"Thank you!" the children roared in unison, followed by the same frenzy as before.

She shook her head as Mr. Munro once again chuckled. "None can say you didn't try, Miss Beaumont."

"But this . . ." She spread her hand toward the assortment of wooden toys, then turned to him. "It is so much. Whyever did you do such a thing?"

He shrugged. "As I said, it is Saint Nicholas Day."

"Which usually entails the giving of sugar plums or dried fruit, not half the inventory of a toy store." She narrowed her eyes. "Is that why you were not able to come earlier this morning? Don't tell me you spent all that time shopping."

He raised his palms in mock surrender. "Guilty as charged."

Warmth spread in her chest, and not just because of the handsome dimple on his right cheek. He'd known the children of Haven House for only a week, and yet he'd thought to bring them gifts for a holiday that usually passed them by empty-handed. It was more than thoughtful. It was the sort of gesture that made a memory—a good one—for children who had too few.

And the sort of thing that made a woman forget she wasn't supposed to fall in love with a man she barely knew.

La! What a ridiculous thought. She tugged the cuffs of her sleeves, resisting the urge to smile like a ninny. "Well, I suppose I cannot very well have you arrested for a crime of generosity."

"I am happy to hear it because I have one last gift." He held out a small box perched atop his palm. "For you."

Her heart thudded against her ribs. Not only was this unexpected, it was beyond the realm of propriety. "I—I dare not accept. It is not seemly."

He laughed, the merry sound of it doing strange things to her heart. "I guarantee you will think otherwise when you see what it is."

Tentatively, she stretched out her fingers, then hesitated, debating if she ought to receive a present from this man or not.

But curiosity won out.

Plucking the tiny wooden box from his hand, she slid open the lid and pulled out a miniature carved animal.

Then blinked at it.

A badger.

She blinked again. He'd given her a badger?

Rafe tensed, every muscle taut as a sail in a headwind. He was mad. That was it. Certifiably insane. He should've recognized his sorry state when he'd first had the idea to gift a woman he barely knew with such an absurdity. What had he been thinking? Ah, but there was the rub. He hadn't been. And still wasn't, especially not with the adorable way Isabelle Beaumont now smiled up at him, amusement shining in her brown eyes.

"Thank you, Mr. Munro. I can honestly say I have never received a badger before." She tilted her head like an inquisitive tot. "I am curious, though, as to why you chose this for me."

"That little fellow," he said, gesturing to the carving nestled in her palm, "reminded me of you. Badgers are fiercely loyal, protective, determined—even when the path ahead looks impossible. They don't yield, not to storms or snares or circumstance. Much like someone I know." His voice dropped just a touch. "Though it's only been a week, you've already faced a great deal, and still you press on. I thought you might like a companion on your desk to remind you what you're made of."

She stared down at the carving, fingers curling around it. When she looked up again, her cheeks were the shade of spring roses, and her smile no longer teased. It was something softer. Something that might stay with him long after he left Haven House today . . . which he ought to do posthaste. He'd missed the morning briefing with Harvey. Forgoing the afternoon meeting would not be wise.

He reset his hat, knocked askew by Jack's earlier assault. "I should be off, but I'll return in the morning. Oh, and I should mention that my mother did contact the aid committee. They were quite moved by your willingness to take on Mrs. Trumble's affairs. You can expect a candidate for a new teacher to arrive on Thursday for an interview."

A dazzling grin lit her face. "That is wonderful! I haven't had time to—"

The playroom door burst open. The Graybills charged in,

Joe wielding a broomstick like a bayonet, and Betty clutching what looked like the remains of Miss Beaumont's bonnet. The children glanced up, but the odd entrance did not hold their attention. Apparently they were used to such quirks from the orphanage caretakers.

"Come quickly, miss!" Joe shook his stick in the air. "The goat's got into the sewing basket."

Next to him, Betty flapped her arms. "And she's eaten all the buttons!"

A crash echoed from somewhere down the corridor, followed by smug bleats.

Miss Beaumont huffed a disgusted sigh. "We don't own a goat. Why is there one in the house?"

Exactly what he'd been wondering. He stifled a grin.

"We do now, miss." Joe puffed out his chest, evidently pleased at acquiring the animal.

"There's no better time than Christmas for a goat," his wife chimed in.

Beside him, Miss Beaumont gripped the badger so tightly that her knuckles blanched, her tension radiating like an August sun. "We cannot care for a goat at the present. You must return it at once."

"Can't." Joe shrugged. "The fellow we got her from said he was Portsmouth bound. Shipping off to America."

Betty bobbed her head. "But we traded him what was left o' the turnips, miss, so ye can be glad o' that."

Rafe glanced at Miss Beaumont. To her credit, she did not go off like a cannon nor did she swoon—both equal contenders for a situation such as this. She merely stood with her chin held high and a calmness to her voice that he doubted she felt. "Yes, Betty, I am happy to be rid of the turnips, but I should like to be rid of the goat as well. Now. Before it eats the curtains. Or the furniture. Or, heaven forbid, one of the children."

Joe frowned. "But—"

"You heard Miss Beaumont," Rafe cut in. He squared his shoulders, a stance that served him well when facing a jury, and employed his most authoritative tone. "But on the off chance that you didn't hear what she said, she asked you to please remove the animal at once. Is that clear?"

Betty wilted along with the bonnet strings in her clutches.

Joe nodded vigorously. "Aye, sir. Right away, then."

He spun on his heel, Betty double-stepping to keep up with him as he strode out the door.

Rafe turned to Miss Beaumont, arching a single brow. "Shall I have my mother ask the committee to send over some candidates for caretakers as well?"

A merry laugh burst from her—pure and unguarded—and she pressed her hands to her lips as if attempting to stifle it. "Oh, Mr. Munro, I am so sorry you had to witness that. But, no, the Graybills may be a handful to manage, yet they mean well. And the children love them dearly, considering them as family."

"As you wish, but the offer remains."

"Thank you," she said, with a glance that felt far warmer than mere gratitude. "Truly."

He dipped his head. "And now I really must be—"

"Mr. Munro!" Cricket darted through a maze of strewn paper and flung his arms around Rafe's legs with enough force to make him stagger.

He reached down to steady the boy, a surprised chuckle escaping his throat. "Easy there, lad."

"Thank you for the little horse!" Cricket beamed up at him, clutching a carved toy to his chest like it was a golden treasure. "I never had a real one before. Not even a pretend one."

Emotion caught in Rafe's throat, and he cleared it roughly. "Well, I'm glad he found the right owner."

"Will you stay, sir? Miss Beaumont is going to lead us in carols. We're to practice for a carol-ade."

"A what?" Rafe cocked his head.

Miss Beaumont laughed. "He means a caroling parade, don't you, Cricket? I promised the children we'd bring Christmas cheer to the neighbourhood after we've learned some songs."

Cricket bounced on his toes. "That's right! So will you stay for the carol-ade practice, Mr. Munro?"

He nearly choked, so much did the boy look like Jenny. Afternoon meeting or not, there was no way he could possibly refuse.

"Yes." He swung the boy in a circle until Cricket could hardly breathe for laughing so heartily.

Miss Beaumont clapped her hands. "Now, children, set down your new toys and gather around the piano. It is time we rehearse our singing."

She sat behind a beat-up box of wood that would serve better as a food trough instead of a musical instrument. And when she struck the first notes of "Hark! The Herald Angels Sing," he winced, fighting the urge to stop up his ears—and the children hadn't even started singing yet. The piano sounded like a tied-up bag of cats screeching to be let out, so off-key did it play.

Cricket entwined his small fingers with his, beaming up at him. "Isn't it grand?"

And that did it.

Not the scarred piano. Not even the dreadful sound of it. But the boy's face—glowing with such pride, such blind satisfaction that what he had was enough.

Rafe's throat closed. Yes, he could purchase them a proper piano. Could even have it delivered before sunset if he wished. But this clenching in his gut wasn't about an instrument. It was about a boy who deserved more than castoffs and charity. A boy who peered up at him like he was some kind of hero.

Like family.

And for the first time, he realized he didn't want to give Cricket a better life just because he might be Jenny's son. Even if it turned out the boy didn't belong to her, Rafe wanted to be a part of his life. And—God help him—he suspected he already was.

EIGHT

"She had a large heart!"
—Charles Dickens, *A Christmas Carol*

Ten days. Ten full days since he'd first inquired about Cricket, and they'd *still* not found one blessed document mentioning the children currently living at Haven House. Rafe rolled his shoulders, then pulled out the last stack of files in the bottom drawer of a now-empty cabinet. Had the records been stored in a different room of the big house? A distinct possibility. One to consider after he and Miss Beaumont finished with this office.

He glanced at her while sinking into a leather armchair, the cushion whooshing on impact. Though it was yet early morning—and a dreary fog-filled one at that—she looked untouched by the gloom, like a lantern newly lit in the mist, her brown eyes agleam as she focused on a portfolio atop her desk. Her trademark scent of ginger and cinnamon offset the musty boxes of paperwork they had yet to sort through. It was a monotonous task, one he'd normally delegate to a clerk, but, oh, how he'd come to enjoy these quiet morns sequestered with the enchanting administrator.

Enjoyed it too much, actually. At first, he'd merely admired the woman's efficiency, her steady drive to bring order to chaos.

But somewhere between misfiled ledgers and tea breaks shared over dusty records, his admiration had deepened into something far less practical. He'd begun to look forward to her laughter, her witty banter, the way she chewed her lip when thinking. It was absurd, really. He was here to uncover the truth about Cricket, not lose his composure over a woman with cinnamon on her skin and a fire in her soul.

Bah!

He flipped open the cover on the top binder. Inside was a tally of missing soup spoons dated 1799. Twenty years ago! Hefting a sigh, he balled the paper and arced it into the bin near the door, destined for the burn barrel out back.

Miss Beaumont glanced over her shoulder. "Another file on the investigation of the missing globe from the schoolroom?"

"No. Misplaced spoons this time—from twenty years ago."

Her gaze drifted to the soon-to-be-overflowing bin. "Well, at least we're making headway on the burn pile."

"And on that file cabinet." He hitched his thumb toward the wooden cabinet nearest a bookshelf. "It's empty now."

"That is good news, though I wish for your sake we could find something of substance." She retrieved a stack of papers tied with twine, then sat next to him in an adjoining chair. The moment she untied the bundle and removed the cover sheet, a huge grin lit her face. "Oh!"

Was this it? Had she found the proverbial needle? He sucked in a breath. "Dare I hope . . . ?"

She pressed her fingers to her lips, pink deepening on her cheeks. "No. Sorry. This has nothing to do with the current orphans, but they are drawings from children of Christmases past. Look." Leaning aside, she offered him several sketches.

He riffled through them, then held one up with a smile. "I particularly like the shading on this goose. It looks properly judgmental."

She laughed. "You would be too if you were sitting in a pot waiting to be cooked."

He shook his head. "Wouldn't happen at my house. We

always eat boar's head stuffed with apples and rosemary for Christmas dinner."

"That sounds lovely."

Not as lovely as you.

The rogue thought ambushed him—unbidden and unchecked. He blinked at the sketch in his hand as if the poorly drawn goose had betrayed him instead of his own untethered feelings.

Handing back the papers, he parried the conversation to her. "And you, Miss Beaumont? What are your Christmas traditions?"

"Naturally there is the pudding." She cut her hand through the air. "Which I daresay most of London partakes of, but I think one of my favorite customs is making pomanders. There's just something magical about the scent of oranges and cloves that makes one feel merry." She bounced on the cushion like one of the children. "But nothing—and I mean nothing—beats snow! Big, fluffy flakes painting the world white and making it new . . . just like our blessed Saviour does for us."

Her voice softened on her last words, whispering of wonder and reverence, and he couldn't help but stare—not at the sketches in her hand, but at her. Something in his chest squeezed. She wasn't just charming about her love of snow; she was luminous in her faith.

"I've never thought of it that way," he said quietly, "but I shall from now on."

"Well, you mayn't get the chance to think anything about it at all, what with the fog and rain we are having." She tipped her head toward the window.

"It's not Christmas yet." He wagged his finger. "And good things come to those who wait."

A laugh trilled out of her. "You sound like the Reverend Mr. Thomas."

"*You* sound like my sister. She was never very patient either."

"Was?" Miss Beaumont arched a brow.

Blast. Why had he brought up Jenny? He blew out a low breath, knowing the truth deep down.

Because it was far too easy to speak with this woman.

"Yes." His fingers tightened on the folder in his lap. "Unfortunately, she died a little over a year ago."

"Ah." It was more of a breath than a word, one accompanied by a spark of keen intelligence in Miss Beaumont's brown eyes. "And she is the mother of the child you seek."

"I believe so. Furthermore"—he met her gaze—"I believe Cricket is that child. He has the same mannerisms. The same pixie-like nose. And his eyes are definitely of Munro stock."

"I cannot say I am surprised. He's quite taken with you—and I have noticed your soft spot for him. There is much to love about that boy." She smoothed the wrinkled papers in her lap. "About all the children, actually. And love is what they need most."

Love. Yes. That was the heart of the matter, was it not? Jenny had loved deeply—privately—and now that love might be all that remained of her. If anyone had seen it, remembered it, he suspected it would be someone like the compassionate woman in front of him. "Tell me, Miss Beaumont, being that you were a teacher at Haven House these past seven years, did you ever have cause to cross paths with Jenny Munro?"

"Jenny Mun—" She gasped, one hand slapping against her chest. "Oh—Jen! How on earth did I never make the connection?"

He smiled, not at her embarrassment but from the adorable shade of red creeping over her cheeks. "Don't be so hard on yourself. You have been a bit preoccupied with putting out fires."

"Still, what a dullard I am!" She flopped back against the cushion. "I guess I only ever called her Jen, never really thinking of her surname." She leaned forward, eagerly meeting his gaze. "Yes, indeed, I did know her. Jen was a quiet soul, so I don't feel like I really got to know her on a personal basis, but she was ever so attentive to the children. She loved to read to them, and she did so faithfully. Came every day to sit among them as if she belonged to them and they to her." Air hissed through her teeth. "And you suspect she is Cricket's mother."

He shrugged. "I cannot say for certain until we find that paperwork."

"Then indeed, we shall!" Rising, she set aside the collection of drawings and dove into a stack on the desk as if sheer conviction might unearth the truth.

And that one small act stirred something in him. Gratitude, certainly, but also something more. Miss Beaumont cared because her heart gave her no other choice. And after all they'd shared for nearly a fortnight now—memories, ideas, laughter over tea and judgmental geese—calling her Miss Beaumont suddenly felt far too distant.

Setting aside his folder, he joined her at the desk. "Miss Beaumont, being that you were on a first-name basis with my sister, I wonder if . . ." His heart thudded, nerves as tightly strung as a schoolboy asking a girl for a first dance.

Pish! He was a man of one and thirty!

He tossed back his shoulders and fingered his lapels. "May I call you Belle, Miss Beaumont?"

She blinked, saying nothing. Not one blessed thing. And that enigmatic look of hers told him absolutely nothing.

Had he crossed a line he ought not have?

"Of course," he backtracked, "if you feel it is inappropriate, then I—"

"No. It's not that."

He frowned. "Then what is it?"

"The thing is . . ." Absently, she ran her finger along the edge of a binder, averting her gaze. "Once we find the document that either proves or disproves your theory about Cricket, you will go back to your life and forget all about Haven House. Forget about me as well."

No bitterness thickened her voice, just dogged certainty, like one who'd seen enough people come and go in her life to know how it all ended.

He dared a step closer. "You think I could forget this place so easily? That I could forget you?" He shook his head. "I don't believe I shall forget either—not in a week or even in a year.

Allow me to call you Belle, Miss Beaumont, not because I mean to leave, but because I mean to stay present—fully—every day I am here, no matter how many days that shall be."

She searched his eyes, only God knowing what went on behind those brown depths, then said at length, "I suppose I cannot turn down such an earnest request by an esteemed barrister like yourself, so . . . yes. You may call me Belle. But only if I may call you Rafe."

"I was hoping you would." He smiled. It was a small triumph, yet sometimes those were sweeter.

The mantel clock chimed, the sound prodding him to spare a glance at the hands. Half past eight? He should've left a half hour ago! He had a morning meeting at nine.

On the other side of town.

He swung about and retrieved his hat and coat from where he'd flung them over a chair, then paused on the threshold. "I'm afraid I must dash. Until tomorrow, then, Belle."

"Kept you too long, did I?" Amusement twinkled in her eyes. "Good day, Rafe."

He strode out with long steps, determined to make that meeting on time. But just before he reached the front door, he stopped. Cricket sat on the bottom step of the grand stairway, arms folded tight, face turned toward the wall, looking as forlorn as a kicked puppy. He didn't even clutch a book as he was so wont to do. Rafe frowned. He could just walk right past the child—for the boy didn't even acknowledge him—and he should. A consultation with a judge was no small thing. But the tug on his heart was too sharp to ignore.

He lowered himself next to the lad. "Bad morning?"

Cricket's knobby shoulders shrugged.

The urge to interrogate the boy surged through his veins, but Rafe waited silently. Such a tactic wouldn't have worked with him when he'd been a child, and he suspected neither would it do the trick with this youngling.

"I said the morning psalm wrong." Cricket spoke so softly, Rafe barely made out the words.

He nudged the boy lightly with his elbow, keeping his tone light. "Everyone says wrong things sometimes. God is ever patient with us in our flounderings."

"But Anne laughed at me!" Cricket's head swiveled, a defiant jut to his little jaw. "She said I don't listen right. She said . . ." His chin dropped to his chest, and the rest came out in a mumble. "She said that's why my mum gave me away."

Anger flared white-hot in Rafe's chest. Oh, the cruelty of children! Crooking a finger, he guided the boy's face upward with a gentle touch. "Anne was wrong," he said firmly.

"Then why din't my mum keep me?" Tears filled those enormous grey-blue eyes. Not a single one fell.

Rafe's heart broke. For the boy. For the ache of all the children who'd inhabited these walls wondering the same thing. For a sister he missed dearly.

But now was not the time to dwell on such melancholies, not with Cricket looking up at him, eyes filled with questions no child this young should have to ponder.

"People do things for all kinds of reasons." Rafe kept his voice steady, a calm in the turbulent sea in which this boy sailed. "But know this, young master—whatever reason led your mother to bring you here was not for lack of loving you. Sometimes love looks like staying. Other times it looks like letting go because it's the only way to keep a loved one safe. Yet none of that—*none* of it—means she stopped loving you. I promise you that."

Cricket's nose scrunched as he angled his head. "Are you sure, sir?"

"Positively. That's what Christmas is about, you know. God's love for us. You see, Cricket, God didn't wait for us to deserve Him. He came to a cold, untidy world and gave everything, not because we were perfect, but because we were precious. So when I tell you that you are loved, it's not just my word. The whole Christmas season says so."

Cricket drew an audible breath.

Then shot to his feet and pounded up the stairs.

"Where are you going?" Rafe called after him.

"To tell Anne it don't matter if I listen right!"

Chuckling, Rafe rose. Apparently he'd set the boy's mind at ease.

But his own whirled at an alarming rate as he dashed to the front door. Now he really would be late. . . .

For a pretrial meeting with none other than Judge Flintwick.

Belle didn't know what rattled her more: the absurd notion that Rafe Munro might actually remember her after all this was over, or the way her name had sounded on his lips.

Belle.

He hadn't used the more formal Isabelle, but the shortened version. The more intimate one. Not that a man had never called her such before, but this time it had felt more like a caress than a name. A promise, almost. A hint of something more, that he'd *like* something more than their simple sorting-through-paperwork morning meetings.

Bish-bosh! What was she thinking? She upped her pace to the front door.

Add to list: Stop letting Rafe's warm voice echo in your head. Focus on the upcoming interview.

Pausing, she pressed her hands along her skirts to remove any wrinkles, then opened the front door with her most businesslike smile—one that froze in place as she took in the straight-backed woman in a black coat who looked as if she'd sucked on lemons for luncheon.

And Father would have scolded her soundly if she let the woman's outward appearance sway her opinion before she got to know her. Belle dipped her head, keeping her smile intact. "Good afternoon. Miss Pringle, I assume?"

The teaching candidate gave a sharp nod, the black feather in her hat bobbing. "I am here to see a Miss Beaumont."

"Please come in." Belle stepped aside, then closed the door

behind Miss Pringle and faced her with a stiff spine, matching the woman's perfect posture. "I am—"

"Miss Beaumont?" A man's gravelly voice turned them both toward the main hall.

Mr. Jabbott, the construction foreman, approached with a hammer in hand, his mouth chiseled into a grim line. "I'm afraid I must have a word with you."

"I shall meet with you straightaway once I am finished with Miss Pringle." Belle fluttered her fingers toward the teacher.

"As you wish, miss." Turning his head, he called over his shoulder, "Pack it up, boys."

What? It wasn't even half past two yet!

"Excuse me a moment, Miss Pringle." Without waiting for a response from the pinch-faced woman, Belle beckoned Mr. Jabbott aside. "You cannot send the men home so early. There is much work to be done."

"That's what I need to talk to you about."

"Very well, but make it quick, please." She cast a glance at Miss Pringle, who stood like a sentinel exactly where she'd left her.

Mr. Jabbott scratched his jaw. "The joists on the south wall are badly charred—far worse than I first thought. They'll have to be replaced instead of bolstered. You'll have to sign off on the cost increase before I can proceed."

"Oh dear. That does sound like a problem."

"And it's not the only one. The heat cracked the plaster in the ceiling above the hearth, and the floorboards near the windows have warped from the water used to douse the flames. Plus, I should mention someone stuffed old newspapers into the chimney flue at some point. Likely worsened the blaze."

Her shoulders sagged. This was turning into a bigger project than she'd imagined.

Add to list: Budget more for plaster, find a new place for old newspapers, and for the love of all that is true and good, check every hearth before lighting a fire.

She faced Mr. Jabbott with more hope than she felt. "I trust you will be finished with all that before Christmas?"

He chuckled. "We'll be lucky to have it done by the end of January."

No! She tossed back her shoulders. "I'm afraid that is unacceptable. Do what you must to have it ready by Christmas Day. I will not have the children crammed into the playroom for such a festive time of year."

"It will cost you." He shrugged.

"Yes, yes. Where is this paper I must sign?"

He pulled a wrinkled invoice from his waistcoat pocket and handed it over.

She scanned the figures, her stomach tightening. It was far more than she'd anticipated. For a moment, doubt whispered. Was this a proper use of the money in her care? But then she pictured the children's faces on Christmas morning, the laughter echoing in that bright, big room with space enough for them to run around. She met the man's gaze. "I'll go sign this straightaway."

"Thank you, miss."

She returned to Miss Pringle, knowing deep down the woman would resent such an interruption to her interview. But so be it.

Miss Pringle sniffed. "Perhaps we ought to reschedule our interview, Miss Beaumont, as you are clearly occupied by other matters."

Belle hid a smirk. Just as she suspected, the woman was clearly put out. "No need to reschedule." She forced a pleasant tone to her voice. Even if the woman was as bristly as a hedgehog, she couldn't afford to lose this teaching candidate. The children needed structure, and with her current administrative duties, that was a luxury she couldn't personally provide. "My office is this way."

She pivoted.

And a clatter rang out, a rumbling sort of clatter accompanied by the sharp clip of half boots hitting the floorboards hard. Betty tore into the front hall, pushing a rickety cart with a dented copper tub atop it. Branches and what might be a curtain sash or two were draped over one side. A string of sausages hung out of her pocket. Soot smudged her left cheek and her chin, and the bottom of her apron hem was smoking.

Belle sighed. Of all the timing! She couldn't help but pop her fists onto her hips. "What is going on?"

Betty shoved her mobcap out of her eyes. "Just tryin' to smoke the meat for dinner, miss. Joe thought we ought to help out, being that Mrs. Bakewell had to dash over to Dr. Mudgeon's office."

"Why is she—no, never mind." Belle folded her arms. She'd have to deal with the cook later. "What is it exactly that *you* mean to do?"

"Why, smoke the meat in the main hall fireplace. Ought not take long, what with it already a-smellin' all char-like." She heaved her weight against the cart.

Belle shot up her hand. "No. You cannot. The men are working in there, and I forbid it."

"Well, it din't work in the schoolroom fireplace, nor the playroom. I think somethin' was living in that one. Birds, I reckon. Possibly bats. Either way, they're out now."

A great screech sounded from above, followed by frantic flapping.

"Leastwise I thought they were out." Betty frowned.

Miss Pringle gasped.

Belle shook her head. What a disaster. As usual. Still, she made sure to keep her tone to a businesslike timbre. "Betty, please return this contraption to wherever you got it from. And for heaven's sake, put the sausages back in the kitchen. No doubt Mrs. Bakewell will manage just fine once she returns."

"Hope so. She left with her bonnet on sideways, mumbling something about her toe bein' broke. Now that I think on it, Joe ought not have left that coal scuttle balanced atop the bread box like he did."

With a great show of gumption, Betty wheeled the cart around and set off down the corridor, sausages swinging and apron still faintly smoking.

Belle stood motionless for a moment, inhaling deeply through her nose and counting to five. Hopefully that would be enough to keep the storm of frustration from escaping through her voice. She turned back to Miss Pringle, mustering a polite smile that felt stitched on. "Now then, Miss Pringle, I am certain we shall have a nice little chat in my office without any more—"

"Miss Beaumont! Miss Beaumont!"

Tibby and Pippin bounded down the staircase like a pair of wild colts and crashed into her, grabbing on to her skirts.

"Children!" Belle grasped the banister to keep from toppling. "What have I said about running indoors?"

"You gotta come right away!" they screeched in unison. "Anne got the kittens stuck in the dumbwaiter, and Jack's broken two broom handles trying to get them out—and they're mewling like they're hurt."

Belle winced. Of course they were. Of course this was happening now.

"I beg your pardon, Miss Beaumont." Miss Pringle tugged her gloves so violently it was a wonder the seams held. "You clearly have . . . responsibilities here well beyond my threshold. I cannot imagine thriving in such an unruly environment. And so I bid you good day." She whirled toward the front door.

"But Miss Pringle!" Belle took a step toward her—then nearly toppled as the twins dragged along with her. "I assure you this is not the way things usually—"

The door slammed.

Belle pressed the heel of her palm to her forehead. Who was she fooling? This was exactly how every day had been since she'd arrived.

And Mr. Snably's offer was sounding better by the minute.

Nine

It is a fair, even-handed, noble adjustment of things, that while there is infection in disease and sorrow, there is nothing in the world so irresistibly contagious as laughter and good-humour.

—Charles Dickens, *A Christmas Carol*

By Friday morning, things had settled into a somewhat quieter routine. Leastwise there hadn't been any more incidents with the kittens, and Mrs. Bakewell was on the mend after suffering the vapors from the Graybills' meat-smoking contraption. Thankfully she hadn't broken her toe. Belle had spent a pleasant morning with Rafe in the office, and she'd even been able to squeeze in a half hour of lessons.

Sighing in relief—mixed with a fair amount of gratitude—Belle dipped a sponge into a dish of water and scrubbed away the arithmetic lesson from the chalkboard. She whispered a quiet prayer of thanks for the calm, recalling the psalmist's words that the Lord "maketh the storm a calm, so that the waves thereof are still." Lunch would be served soon and—

"Miss!"

Stomping feet pounded loud. Joe burst through the door, coat misbuttoned and hair mussed. He held up his hands as if she were a Bow Street runner come to serve him a writ. "We din't have nothing to do with it, I swear."

Betty clattered in behind him, cheeks flushed. "Joe's right. It weren't us!"

Wonderful. Now what?

Belle set down her sponge and folded her hands in front of her, forcing a calm tone. "Perhaps you could tell me exactly what it is that does not involve you?"

"In the playroom. Come along." With a leap, Joe hooked his arm through hers and tugged her from the schoolroom.

Belle disengaged from him just before descending the stairs, for surely they'd both have tumbled into an inglorious heap on the landing.

Bypassing the pounding of hammers in the main hall, she followed Joe into the playroom, then stopped hardly past the threshold. Three hulking porters were in the final stages of pulling off the hessian sacking from an upright piano. Its polished case caught the late-morning light streaming through the window, gleaming like an unwrapped secret—one that stole her breath. The children ran past her squealing, nearly knocking her off balance.

"Right, then!" Joe slapped his hands together, edging toward the door with Betty close behind. "We'll just pop off. Best not to get in the way o' professional men at work."

And with that the Graybills scurried away, abandoning Belle to manage the mysterious delivery on her own. Leave it to them to think themselves in trouble for a blessing such as a new piano.

Tibby clapped her hands. "A real piano!"

"Do you think it's from Mr. Munro?" Anne called as she dragged the old piano stool away from the monstrosity of the off-key instrument in the corner.

"I think it's from me." Pippin jabbed his thumb against his chest, earning a chorus of snorts.

Belle could only stand frozen, too many thoughts swirling to seize hold of any one in particular.

Two of the burly porters passed her by with a respectful tip of their hats, heaps of sacking stowed beneath their thick arms. The third approached, pulling a small lead holder from his pocket and offered it, along with a stiff board wrapped in string that secured several sheets of paper. "If you'd be so good as to acknowledge receipt, miss, we'll be on our way."

She held up her hand, staving off the waybill. "I beg your pardon, but there must be some mistake. I did not order a piano. I am afraid you will have to recall your men and remove it."

"Can't."

"Why not?"

"Says right here this pianoforte's been bought and paid for by a Mr.—" He squinted at the paper. "Munro."

She inhaled sharply. Anne *had* guessed correctly. Not that it was a complete stretch of the imagination, but still . . .

Her gaze drifted back to the polished case, the warm light skipping over the keys. Beautiful. Even so, she frowned. Not that she'd never received generous gifts before—for she was standing beneath the roof of one right now. But this felt different. More personal. More . . . tender.

And that was what unsettled her most.

There had been a time years ago when another man measured everything in terms of worth and advantage. Would she never be free of Ben's shadow? But no. He'd marked her in ways she couldn't shake. Ben had calculated love like a ledger, as though kindness could be weighed against ambition, and she'd continually come up short in his eyes.

But surely this was not that!

As far as she knew, Mr. Munro hadn't done any weighing or calculating. He hadn't done this to impress her or to advance his own interest. He'd simply seen a need and filled it. And that—heaven help her—was infinitely more dangerous. A grand gesture could be dismissed as theatre, but the sort of man who gave without fanfare or expectation? Well. That was the sort of man who could steal a woman's heart before she even knew it was gone.

Her throat tightened as the children swarmed around the instrument, no longer able to resist banging on the keys. Belle pressed a hand to her middle, willing her thoughts back to safer ground instead of the heartwarming gift given by a man who freely gave of his wealth, his time . . . himself. A man whose presence was supposed to be temporary, yet with each small kindness he carved a deeper place in her heart as a companion she wasn't sure she ever wanted to give up.

Add to list: Stop entertaining notions that don't belong in an orphanage—or in my heart.

"I'm afraid I have other deliveries to make today, miss." The porter jabbed the board into her hands. "So if ye'll please sign?"

She drew in a slow breath as she wrote her signature. "Thank you."

After tucking the document into a large coat pocket, the man offered a polite nod. "Good day and enjoy the new piano."

Anne shoved Jack off the stool. "I know 'Silent Night.' Let me play."

"Hey!" Jack shouted.

"I know 'Joy to the World'!" Cricket tossed aside his worn copy of *Goody Two-Shoes* and darted forward, clambering on top of Anne's lap. "I can play it. I can show you—look!"

"Cricket, no! You're doing it wrong." Anne pushed him away, and the boy landed on the worn floorboards at Jack's feet.

Jack towered over him, fists on his hips. "You don't know anything, Cricket. Go play blocks with Rory and Birdie, where you belong."

The bright hope on Cricket's face vanished as he rose. He stuffed his hands into his pockets and wandered to the window seat, shoulders hunched. Silently, he curled against the wall with his knees to his chest, the crown of his head barely visible above the sill.

Thoroughly breaking Belle's heart.

The others didn't notice this silent shadow. Cricket didn't cry. Didn't sulk. But there was something ominous about his stillness—something far too quiet for a boy of only five summers.

Ignoring the chaos at the new piano, Belle approached him, wondering not for the first time how often a child had to be overlooked before he started to believe he was invisible.

A man's life ought not be dependent upon paperwork, and yet such was the nature of English justice. In the shadows of early evening, Rafe eyed the fat portfolio on the coach seat next to him, rubbing his chin. It would be a late one tonight, which was exactly why he'd left the office. A quick stop at Haven House, a quicker check on the renovation progress at his own home, then he'd settle in with a large pot of stout black tea in the comfort of his own study.

The coach stopped, and he alighted, surprised at the spring in his step as he approached the orphanage. With so many late nights, he'd been battling fatigue, yet just the thought of seeing Belle and Cricket had a way of enlivening him.

He rang the bell. Moments later, the door opened—and there stood Belle.

Even exhausted, she was beautiful. But tonight, her weariness was more pronounced. A few wisps of hair clung to her temples and broke loose behind her ears, her usually polished chignon a bit worse for the wear. The shadows beneath her eyes were deeper and the crease between her brows prominent instead of faint, as if she held too many burdens too close. Still, the warmth of her brown eyes softened when her gaze met his.

"Mr. Munro—I mean, Rafe." One of her brows rose slightly, but the tease lacked its customary spark. "You're a little early for our daily paperwork session . . . by twelve hours."

"You know what they say, twelve hours early is right on time." He grinned. "But that's not why I came. I merely wanted to make sure the piano arrived safe and sound?"

"It did, and you are now the hero of Haven House. The children have been singing your praise all day—literally. Would you like to come in and see it?" She stepped aside, making room for him to enter.

But he merely shook his head. "I can see it in the morning, thank you. I don't want to intrude on your dinnertime."

"We've already eaten. The children were famished after practicing carols for several hours."

"And yet it appears to be all quiet now. Don't tell me you slipped a bit of laudanum in with their broth?"

She laughed. "No, they are merely upstairs playing funeral vigil with the Graybills. It's not one of my favorite pastimes for them, but on days like this, I selfishly covet the silence. And, truth be told, the children adore Joe and Betty. The pair have a knack for turning the simplest games into grand adventures."

He chuckled softly, studying her face in the golden glow of the entry lamps. She carried this place on her shoulders—and it was showing. She deserved more than just a few moments to herself. And heaven knew he could use a reprieve himself before digging into page upon page of depositions.

On impulse, he offered his arm. "Then perhaps I can persuade you to steal a bit more silence. There's a Christmas market only a few streets over. Nothing elaborate, but you look as if you could do with some night air, and I know I could. You'd be doing me a favor, actually. One can only take the Inns of Court for so long without going a bit batty."

She narrowed her eyes. "I don't think anyone could ever accuse you of anything but unflappable composure."

"Even barristers need an occasional escape from their own minds . . . and I would rather spend that reprieve in your company."

Her breath caught faintly, but she gathered herself with a soft chuckle. "Very well. I suppose I owe you at least that much."

After she gathered her coat and bonnet, they set off on foot, leaving the coachman with instructions to wait and promising he wouldn't be long. December air nipped with a cool bite as they strolled the few streets to the market, where braziers and lanterns burned brightly. Vendors of all manner hawked roasted chestnuts, ribbons, sugared almonds, and sprigs of holly. The scents of savory meat pies and spiced apples filled the air, and somewhere near the edge of the crowd, a fiddler scratched out "The Holly and the Ivy" with a merry lilt.

But Rafe was more interested in the woman at his side, her face flushed rosy from the cool air. She paused at one of the toy stalls, her gloved hand brushing over a small wooden ark set. Tiny pairs of carved animals trotted up a ramp to the hull. She quickly stepped away, but not before he caught a certain longing in her expression.

He guided her back with a light touch and pulled out his coin purse. "For the children, of course."

"Rafe, no." She pressed her fingers to his hand. "We've only just received the piano today. You cannot spoil them so thoroughly."

"Nonsense." He offered the coin to the merchant. "They—and you—need an ark to weather storms. It's a necessity."

She shook her head, biting her lip, and that small gesture nearly undid him.

"It's a lovely thing," she admitted quietly.

"Yes." His voice lowered without quite meaning to. "It is."

And for a breath too long, neither of them looked at the ark.

Once the toy was packaged in brown paper and twine, Rafe tucked it beneath his arm, and they reentered the bustle. Belle's arm brushed against his sleeve, just enough to send a ripple of awareness through him, and he caught her glancing sideways at him.

"What?" he asked.

"Just that . . . well, if you continue purchasing gifts at this pace, Haven House may need to add on a second wing simply to hold them."

"I should like to think I'm merely investing in the children's future, not ornamenting a building. Those young ones have had trouble enough in their few years, and if parting with a few coins makes them happy, then so be it."

"You do realize that's quite a dangerous thing to say to a woman like me, do you not? I am the director of an orphanage, after all, and words like that might endear you to me most handily."

"That is a risk I am willing to take." He winked.

"You are incorrigible, sir." She laughed. "But we really should be getting back."

He guided her around a cart selling sticks of sugar flavored with peppermint oil, her step noticeably lighter as they retraced their route.

"I think this outing has done us both good," he observed.

"Agreed. And I thank you for it." She smiled up at him.

Just a simple smile. Nothing more. Yet it was enough to shrink the distance between them. His hand hovered next to hers, their gloves brushing now and again as they walked. Too close.

But not nearly close enough.

He ought to have been thinking about the case—the interviews left undone, the affidavits and depositions, the man waiting for justice. Instead, he was here. With her. There was no use pretending otherwise—tonight it would not be case files occupying his mind, but this woman, and the way her gaze had dared linger, like a touch not quite given.

One he suddenly desperately wanted.

Ten

> "You may—the memory of what is past half makes me hope you will—have pain in this."
>
> —Charles Dickens, *A Christmas Carol*

Rafe huffed a sharp sigh as he tossed aside the last worthless file filled with a collection of goose-grease remedies into the empty box on the floor. The once-cluttered office of Mrs. Trumble now felt like a broken promise, empty and hollow. Dust outlined where ledgers had once sat on the bookshelves. No more leaning towers of crates stood about. Every cabinet drawer was barren, and even the desk where Belle resided had been cleared of its stacks. Nothing but the faint scent of old ink and lavender water hung about, like a ghost unwilling to leave.

He pinned his gaze—and last hope—on Belle. "Please tell me that after a fortnight of searching, you hold the children's records in your hands."

She traced the edge of one document with her fingertip, her brows faintly knitting as her gaze bounced between the two.

Dare he hope?

But then her lips flattened.

And she set the papers on the desk.

"I'm sorry, Rafe." Genuine compassion thickened her voice.

He sank back in the leather chair, unwilling to hold hands with defeat. Clearly the former administrator had no archival sense whatsoever. Other than a gut feeling and Cricket's striking grey-blue Munro eyes, Rafe had a sinking realization he might never know for certain if the child had belonged to Jenny.

As if summoned by misfortune, Betty and Joe Graybill stumbled through the open office door, bouncing off one another like marbles in a child's game. Why Belle insisted on keeping the incompetent duo was a wonder. They'd single-handedly frightened off three teaching prospects to date. Naturally she felt a loyalty to Mrs. Trumble's servants, but there had to be a point when enough was enough . . . hadn't there?

"Pardon, miss, sir." Joe waved a red-checked handkerchief in the air.

Rafe stifled a groan. "Is that a flag of surrender, or are you signaling a new emergency?"

Betty batted her husband's arm down. "No, no. Just lookin' for that box o' candle stubs, we are. Wondered if ye'd seen 'em?"

Belle frowned. "Candle stubs?"

"Aye, miss." Joe tucked the cloth into his waistcoat. "Mrs. Trumble always kept a supply o' candles with her private papers in case o' emergency. Bein' ye've been poking about her whatnots, we wondered if ye'd seen 'em. There's a blizzard on the way, and we thought to have them at the ready."

Belle swept her hand toward the dust motes dancing in a rather spectacular beam of sunshine through the window. "There is more danger of swooning from the heat than snow today."

"Heat?" Betty gasped, then cuffed Joe on the shoulder. "That's right! That was why the missus moved 'em last summer—said the sun kept melting the wax on her important papers. Had you put it in the cellar, remember?" The woman beamed as if she'd brought a murderer to justice.

"*Important* papers?" Rafe jumped to his feet, wild with hope. "Where is the cellar?"

"Pish, won't do ye no good to go nosin' down there." Joe

blew air through his lips. "Too much water leakin' in, making everything green about the gills. That box o' candles and papers were moved to the main hall last fall."

"Oh dear." Belle slapped a hand to her chest. "That's where the fire was."

A brick sank in Rafe's gut. Hard.

"But," Betty cut in, tapping her lower lip, "as I recall, last winter it were trundled off to the missus's wardrobe."

"'Til the moths got too thick." Joe scratched his jaw. "On second thought, ne'er shoulda used treacle to kill the flutterin' devils."

And Rafe could take it no longer. "Blast it! Where is this box now?"

Betty snapped her fingers. "Why, 'tis in the scullery. Behind the potato bins. Thanks fer yer help, sir. Ye've a mind bright as a penny, ye do."

He exchanged a glance with Belle, and without a word, they rushed past the Graybills.

But the Graybills followed.

"Mind the pail!" Joe called behind them as Belle narrowly dodged a tipped-over mop bucket in the corridor.

Rafe grabbed hold of her hand for the rest of the way, just in case there were any other ankle-threatening obstacles.

"Don't let the door stick!" Betty called as Belle reached for a latch near the kitchen. "It's got a hinge that grabs when the weather's about to change, such as with the blizzard coming."

Ignoring them, Rafe darted into the cramped scullery, inhaling herbs and dirt. Large sacks sat on the floor. Crates of root vegetables lined one wall. Various dried bundles of greens hung from the low ceiling.

"Over there." Belle pointed.

In two strides, Rafe shoved aside a tall bin of potatoes and retrieved the box behind it, lid askew. A spider scurried along the baseboards, earning a squeak out of Belle while a few potatoes rolled across his shoes from his own surprise.

Belle stepped over to the worktable and cleared away some

bowls. "I certainly hope this is it. I cannot bear to think of other hidey-holes in which the Graybills may have stowed Mrs. Trumble's records."

Without wasting another breath, Rafe pulled off the lid. Inside, amidst a jumble of candle stubs, lay a thick file of folders tied with a red ribbon, melted wax globbed on parts of it. As much as he yearned to yank out the bundle—and though it killed him in every possible way—he stepped back. "As director of Haven House, it is only right you examine what is in the box."

She smiled. "Then I shall do so with all haste."

The Graybills snatched up the candles with a considerable hubbub, then dashed off as Belle untied the ribbon and picked up the first folder. Once opened, her eyes lit. "It's the information on the twins!" She reached for another. "And Jack."

His heart stuttered as she glanced through each successive binder, then stopped completely as she opened the last one—and her brows drew into a serious line. Her head shook slightly, and a low murmur passed her lips. "I . . . I don't understand."

Her face lifted to his, sorrow swimming in her eyes. "I'm sorry, Rafe. All that's in Cricket's folder is . . . this."

She held up a gold chain. A cross pendant dangled from it. With a pearl at its center.

Of course men showed emotion—generally in their own stoic fashion. Belle could still remember the way her father had turned aside to wipe his eyes as the church bells tolled for her mother's burial. His back had been rigid, his shoulders squared, but that single, surreptitious swipe had spoken volumes. Wholly understandable, naturally.

But this?

Rafe's Adam's apple bobbed, his hand stretching with a tremor for the necklace. His face, usually so composed, lost all pretense of control.

"May I?" The words came out raspy.

She could no more deny him had he asked her for the moon.

"Of course." She laid the pendant in his palm, her fingers brushing his—a touch that sent a shiver up her arm.

His fingers clasped the pendant reverently, and he held it to his chest like a prayer. For a long while, he said nothing.

"You . . . are familiar with this piece of jewelry?" She spoke softly, loathing to intrude upon whatever memories he wandered in.

"It—" His voice cracked.

Then with a great inhale and larger exhale, Rafe Munro snapped back into character, the no-nonsense barrister one wouldn't dream of catching off-guard, or with his bleeding heart in plain view.

But Belle had seen it. For one brief, sacred moment, he had allowed himself to be vulnerable in front of her. Her! Of all people. A quiet warmth blossomed in her chest for the strange and unexpected honour. He'd trusted her, if only for a heartbeat, with a piece of his soul.

"This"—he suspended the cross from his fingers—"is my sister's."

"So Cricket *is* your nephew," she breathed.

Then doubt assailed her, and she pulled her gaze from the pendant to the man. "But how can you be certain? A necklace isn't the written word. It could have been lost. Sold. Stolen. How do you know it belongs to your sister and that she meant it to be in that folder?"

"The details align too precisely for this to be happenstance." Rafe's jaw tensed, but his tone remained calm. "Shortly before Jenny decided to volunteer here daily, she went away for six months to what I was told was a finishing school . . . which I now suspect was really a home for unwed mothers. She was never the same after she returned, and no wonder if she'd borne a child and put that babe in the care of Mrs. Trumble."

"Why would there be no paperwork, then? Why only a necklace?"

"You know as well as I what a shame such a thing would bring on a family like mine. If my father—or anyone of rank—had discovered the truth, Jenny would have been cast out entirely. The only way to protect both herself and the child was to leave no official record. No names. No guardianship documents. Only Mrs. Trumble's discretion and a token should she wish to ever reclaim the babe as her own." He lifted the pendant once more, the gold cross gleaming in the faint light of the scullery. "This was the only token Jenny could safely leave. Something unmistakable to the family. Perhaps she hoped that someday things might change. I don't know."

Belle didn't either. Oh, how she longed for Mrs. Trumble's wisdom in this matter! And just like that, a fresh wave of grief washed over her, sinking in her belly. She pressed her fingers to her middle. "Not that I don't believe you, Rafe, because I do, but as administrator—and a newly minted one at that—I am not certain I can simply release Cricket to you just because of a necklace."

"Then allow me to put your mind at ease." His shoulders straightened as if delivering an argument in a courtroom. "In law, there is such a thing as circumstantial evidence—that which, though indirect, carries weight when supported by reason. The child's age, his very features, match what I know. And this pendant—which was never meant to leave my sister's possession—speaks louder than any paper. Were I arguing this before Chancery, I would say the preponderance of evidence lies in my favor."

The urge to press for firmer proof warred with the empty file on the worktable. What proof was there in matters like these? Everything he said made sense—painfully so. Besides, he wouldn't need proof if he adopted the child outright. And glancing at the pendant once more, seeing the hope it represented for Cricket and Rafe, she could not refute the quiet conviction settling in her soul.

A genuine smile tugged her lips. For him. For the boy. This *was* good. Right. True. Cricket would have the family he so deserved. A home of his own. A loving uncle to dote on him. His days of being bullied by the older children would be over.

And yet, in a layer beneath her happiness, a small hollow opened in her chest. This would be the end, wouldn't it? No more mornings with this man. No more shared cups of tea or commiserating about the Graybills' antics. Once Rafe claimed his nephew, his ties to Haven House would be severed. He would return to his life—his world—and she would remain here. A selfish ache squeezed her chest, one she could not deny.

Nor one she would admit.

She widened her smile. "Well then, congratulations, Rafe. You are an uncle! And there could be no better nephew than our little Cricket to welcome into your life, though I suppose you will have to make some accommodations before you take him home."

"Yes, I—"

"Pardon, miss." Mrs. Bakewell poked her head into the scullery. "Betty told me there's a gent in the front hall to see you."

"Thank you, Mrs. Bakewell." She turned back to Rafe.

But he was already stepping aside so she could pass. "I'll see you to the door. I should be at the office by now, anyway."

They wound through the corridors, accompanied by the sound of childish laughter and stomps from upstairs.

Mr. Snably paced near the front door, a leather portfolio under one arm. At their approach, he offered a warbly "Good morning, Miss Beaumont," and an awkward dip of his head toward Rafe. "To you as well, sir."

Belle's brow scrunched. "I didn't realize we had an appointment, Mr. Snably. Forgive me if I've forgotten. It's been a bit . . . hectic around here."

Add to list: Remember to check the scheduling diary before the day begins. And stock up on handkerchiefs for when Cricket—and Rafe—leave Haven House.

"Nothing of the sort." Mr. Snably wagged his head. "I have arrived quite unannounced, but I don't think unwelcome. Leastwise not after you see this." He handed over the portfolio.

"That looks rather legal," Rafe murmured.

It was. She nearly choked when her eyes landed on the

amount now being offered for Haven House. This was no mere inquiry but a full proposal of purchase. And when her gaze drifted lower, to the signature of the prospective buyer, her breath caught.

No!

It couldn't be.

She jerked her gaze back to Mr. Snably, one hand to her throat. "Is this correct? Did you meet with the man who signed this?"

He shook his head. "Mr. Smallbone delivered that document to my office but an hour ago, and being he said the matter was quite urgent, I felt you should be made aware of it at once. May I say, Miss Beaumont, you look positively green—which is understandable. Money like that isn't offered every day. Perhaps I should come back later, after you've had time to digest the information?"

"Yes," Rafe answered for her, taking her arm. "Good day, Mr. Snably." He guided her to a nearby bench while the man saw himself out.

She couldn't bring herself to meet Rafe's eyes. It felt wrong, somehow. Everything did. The folder was heavy in her hands, the signature searing through the paper like a brand. Of all the people in all the world, why him?

Why now?

"Are you quite all right?" Gently, Rafe pressed his hand against hers. "Shall I call for Betty or Mrs. Bakewell to bring you a cup of tea?"

"I . . . no. I am fine." She drew a fortifying breath.

"You don't look it. What has you so rattled? I can only assume from what I heard that you've been given some sort of monetary offer for Haven House and that whoever is making the offer is someone you know. Or . . . fear, perhaps?"

"Fear?" She laughed bitterly. "I suppose nowadays some do, particularly those who are indebted to him."

Rafe's gaze sharpened. "Who is he?"

She swallowed. Then forced her gaze to Rafe's—and the

kindness she found there nearly undid her. "Ebenezer Scrooge," she murmured.

His brow furrowed. "*The* Ebenezer Scrooge? The heartless scoundrel who's teamed up with Jacob Marley?"

"The very one." Her throat tightened.

"But . . . how do you know him? You are all that is light and good. From what I've heard of the man, he's as dark as they come."

She shifted uncomfortably on the wobbly wooden bench. Should she tell him? If she did, what would he think of her?

Yet why should that matter? She was a grown woman. An administrator. Director of an orphanage, for goodness' sake.

Even so, her voice barely rose above a whisper. "I was young. So was he. Ben wasn't always as you've heard. There was kindness in him once, and ambition—but not the kind that devours. Or, well, perhaps I was too blind to see that at the time."

Rafe said nothing, just waited.

"We met when I was little more than seventeen," she continued. "He was apprenticed to one of my father's business associates, a Mr. Fezziwig." Her lips curved into a bittersweet smile. "Ben was full of dreams and determination, and I believed in him. He proposed, and we made plans for a future."

She stared at the folder in her hands, blood turning cold. "But he changed. His love for me—if there ever was such—dwindled. He cared only for gain. The more wealth he amassed, the more he feared losing it. I watched him harden until finally I could reach him no more. So . . ." She drew in a shaky breath. "I broke off the engagement, and he did not try to stop me."

"He was a fool," Rafe said harshly.

"Perhaps." She blinked back a sting of tears. "Or perhaps I was for believing in him in the first place. And now . . . well, now he wishes to purchase Haven House."

"What on earth would he want with an orphanage?"

"I don't know." She shook her head. "But Ben does nothing without reason. There's something he wants—I just don't know what that is yet."

Eleven

You fear the world too much.
—Charles Dickens, *A Christmas Carol*

Late. Again. Rafe jumped from his carriage before the driver pulled the horses to a full stop, his heels striking the stone with a thud. Blast! He should be at the office right now. This tardiness had to stop. Such negligence would lose the Grindlethorn case.

But this couldn't wait.

He yanked open the front door of his town house, bellowing for his mother the moment he entered. Pulling off his hat, he sidestepped a workman hunched on the floor, nailing in a new baseboard. The scent of cut wood and fresh varnish hung in the air. Rafe crossed the hall, avoiding a toolbox and a ladder, his heart hammering nearly as hard as the thud of the carpenter's mallet.

"Mother?" he called again, pitching his voice down the hallway as he strode toward the breakfast room. Surely she'd be there. She always lingered at this hour, nursing her tea, writing notes to friends—the same quiet habits she'd clung to since Jenny's death.

His mother glanced up from the morning news as he charged into the room. Concern puckered her brow, and she set the paper aside. "You look as though you've outrun the post coach. What has happened?"

He pulled up a chair beside her, taking one of her hands. He might as well be cradling a sparrow, so delicate were her bones. Would this news crush her, or would it bring a surge of life to this woman who grieved so deeply?

"There is something I need to tell you," he said quietly.

Her fingers tensed. "Has someone died?"

"Nothing of the sort. I bear good news. Wonderful news, actually."

"That's a relief." She pulled away, took a sip of tea, then settled against the chair, apparently ready for a lively tale. "Well then, what is it?"

He rose and paced in front of the buffet, unsure how to tell her what he knew without upsetting her with talk of Jenny—which was what bringing her up usually accomplished. It was a strain to collect words like dandelion puffs floating in the wind, but he must. And quickly, or she'd be alarmed again.

He took a stance near the window, the December sun casting pale ribbons across the floorboards. "Do you remember when Jenny insisted on attending that finishing school, despite your objections about her traveling so far from home and Father's scoffing that she seemed finished well enough for him?"

"Of course I do." His mother toyed with the string of pearls at her neck. "But why bring that up now?"

"It is my belief she never attended such a school and instead she went to a home for women in a delicate situation."

Mother's eyes narrowed. "What sort of situation?"

Gah! His ears turned hot. What a muddle he was making.

He reclaimed his seat with a heavy plop. "What I'm trying to tell you is Jenny went away to birth a child, then she put that babe into the care of Mrs. Trumble at Haven House. That's why when Jenny returned home, she spent so much time at the orphanage. To be part of the boy's life."

"Don't be absurd, Rafe."

"You know that is not one of my usual traits."

"But—" The word broke like a brittle bone. His mother jerked upright, her eyes wide and unblinking. For a moment she simply stared, lost somewhere between disbelief and something far more fragile. Then her chest rose with a sharp breath, and one hand flew to her throat. "It cannot be."

The words came out strangled.

A surge of pity warred with frustration inside him. She was grieving still, and now this truth tore at wounds barely scabbed over. Ripped off by him. But pity could not change facts.

Nor could it shield an innocent child.

"It is true. I have seen the boy myself." The image of Cricket's grey-blue eyes burned bright in his mind. And that laugh . . . When Cricket laughed, it set to rights all that was ugly about life. How to explain that, though? Somehow the boy had slipped into a small alcove in his heart and made himself fully at home.

And every visit to Haven House made that space wider.

Rafe leaned forward. "He's a charming lad, Mother. The boy will fill your days and these rooms with laughter."

"No." The word clipped out of her as sharp as the snip of gardening shears, such vitriol making no sense whatsoever.

He cocked his head. "What do you mean 'no'?"

"Even if what you say is true, your sister was right in what she did. We cannot accept the consequence of an improper liaison with a common soldier."

He threw up his hands. "What soldier?"

Mother reached for her half-drunk cup of tea but did not bring it to her lips. She merely stared into the liquid as if some sort of drama were stirring in that tepid drink. "If what I suspect is true," she murmured, "then it would have been Daniel Prescott. An ensign stationed briefly at Woolwich, just after his return from Spain. He was introduced to your sister at Lady Hensley's musicale."

Daniel Prescott. Rafe turned the name around in his mind, examining it from all sides. Nothing about it was familiar. "I don't recall Jenny ever speaking of him. Nor you."

"There was little to tell." She shifted the cup in her hands, her gaze never quite lifting. "Like so many at that time, he was a young man of your sister's acquaintance, eager, full of talk of commissions and adventure. She was enchanted the first night she met him and rushed home to tell me. I let her know in no uncertain terms that this was not a relationship to be pursued and put a stop to it immediately. Or so I thought."

"But you think this Prescott is the father." Leaning back in his chair, Rafe scrubbed his knuckles along his jaw. Daniel Prescott, a name without a face. A man who'd taken advantage of his sister. His hands curled into fists.

Still, Cricket had a father—which ought not be such a surprise. It was just that . . . well, after spending time with the boy, *he'd* hoped to fill that place in his life. But with a military man for a sire, no doubt the lad would leave London—if the man wanted him, that is.

A long sigh leaked out of him. "This Prescott must be told, of course."

"Impossible." His mother set down her cup. "A letter came for your sister scarcely a month after Ensign Prescott shipped out. He died of dysentery, she said. She never spoke of him again, so I assumed—wrongly, it seems—that nothing had come of their acquaintance."

But it had. And how the deuce had Rosamund Munro not noticed any change in her own daughter's body? Rafe studied his mother. Pregnancy left its signs. How could she have missed such a telltale condition? "And you suspected nothing?"

She shook her head. "Would that I had, but no. Your sister kept her secret well hidden. But now her insistence on that—that *finishing* school makes all the sense in the world."

Rafe vaguely recalled those months. There had been some tense moments and even a night of raised voices, but he'd been too busy with preparing for the bar, memorizing precedents and the finer points of law. Too consumed by his own ambitions to notice what his sister might have been carrying beneath layers of loose muslin.

Absently, he tapped one finger against the tabletop. "And yet there is still the matter of a young boy in desperate need of a family—our family, it seems, if this Prescott is dead."

"No, Rafe." His mother's voice dipped low. Leaning close, she clutched his arm. "You must see the danger here. The boy's existence—the situation of his birth—changes everything. If the truth were ever whispered beyond these walls, what do you think society would say? What scandal would attach to your sister's name even in death? And to ours?"

He jerked from her grasp is if she'd burned him. "He is a child, Mother! An innocent. Society be hanged!"

"Society is not so easily silenced, my son, and I am terrified of what cruelty they would heap upon his head—and yours. The ton has no mercy. None. Even the gentlest rumour could undo everything. Your sister tried so hard to spare that child from such a fate." Her voice warbled with emotion. "I will not see her sacrifice torn apart by gossip."

He stared at her, seeing not judgment now but true fear and grief etched deep into the lines at the sides of her eyes. Slowly, he shook his head. "You would have me abandon the boy simply to shield him from wagging tongues?"

"I would have you protect what your sister loved." Tears welled shiny in her eyes. "The boy is safe where he is. Please . . . let that be enough."

The last slant of afternoon sun vanished as Belle stepped into the familiar sitting room of her father's house. She tugged off her gloves with a soft sigh, not because twilight would soon encroach but because the day had been so splendidly bright. And with but eleven days remaining until Christmas, each cloudless sky seemed to mock her dwindling hopes for snow.

Add to list: Pray more fervently for fluffy flakes. Perhaps even consider asking the Graybills to come up with some sort of snow-making contraption.

Ack! Was she truly that desperate?

"My sweet girl, Hannah told me you were here."

She turned at the sound of her father's voice and welcomed his embrace.

When he pulled back, he eyed her with an arched brow. "How did you know I'd be home from the office early today?"

"I didn't." She smiled. "But sometimes a daughter simply needs her father and hopes Providence arranges the rest. As it turns out, Providence was kind today."

"Hmm. Need?" With a light touch, he directed her to the sofa while he took an adjacent chair. "I hope all is well at Haven House?"

"The main hall is still in a shambles, though the workmen are pressing on—far too slowly for my liking, however. The Graybills haven't increased the menagerie they've already brought in . . . unless you count the owl they are now supposedly nursing back to health in the potting shed. And the children are all healthy, if rambunctious. I may be going deaf in one ear from their robust carol practicing. So, yes, I would say things are well—for the moment."

He folded his hands, steepling only two fingers and tapping them against his chin. "Then why are you here instead of there?"

Good question. She should be able to figure this out on her own, especially since she was the one in charge of Haven House, and yet . . . well, was there not merit in seeking the counsel of a wise man? And her father was the wisest man she knew.

Save for Rafe Munro, of course. But she couldn't very well call on him.

She toyed with her gloves, arranging them flat on her lap and smoothing out invisible wrinkles. "I have recently received an offer for Haven House. A rather substantial one."

"How substantial?"

She glanced up. "Twelve thousand pounds."

A sharp whistle slipped past his lips. "Twelve—gracious, Belle! Who would pay that much for an orphanage?"

Immediately, she snapped her gaze back to her gloves, fingers fussing with a button that needed no adjusting. This would not go over well.

"Ben," she said barely above a whisper.

The name was like flint striking stone, lighting a fire beneath her father. He hurtled from his chair, pacing to the mantel with a dark mutter. "That heartless rogue—scoundrel! Of all the nerve." He wheeled about, his face flushed and jaw set like a steel trap. "What could that penny-pincher possibly want with Haven House? Don't tell me this is some kind of twisted revenge for you turning down his suit all those years ago, or I swear I shall—"

She quickly raised a hand. "No, Father. I doubt he knows I'm even involved. Thus far only our solicitors have been in communication."

The deep colour that had risen up his neck eased to a more natural hue as he exhaled and resumed his seat. "I see," he said, though skepticism yet lingered in his eyes. "But again, why would a skinflint like Scrooge wish to purchase an orphanage for such an exorbitant price? It makes no sense."

"It makes no sense to me either, a mystery I would dearly love to understand."

Her father rubbed his palm along his thigh. "I do not want you tangled up with that man. Not again." He pursed his mouth a moment. "Say, what about this barrister friend of yours? Could you ask Mr. Munro to make some discreet inquiries about what ol' Scrooge might be up to?"

The very mention of Rafe created a strange flutter in her chest. Though she'd only known him a short amount of time, they were already friends, and she had no doubt he'd comply. She need only ask. But it wouldn't be fair of her. Not now. Not with this morning's revelation of Cricket being his nephew and the big murder case he was soon to represent. She could not in good conscience allow him to take on one more thing.

She set her gloves aside on the cushion before she strangled the life out of the fabric. "I am certain Rafe would investigate if I brought the matter before him, but he is quite occupied at the moment. I don't feel right about increasing his burden."

"*Rafe*, is it?" He waggled his eyebrows.

Heat rushed to her cheeks. "Father, stop it."

He chuckled, thoroughly enjoying her discomfort. "What? Is it so wrong to hope my daughter finds love and happiness? He is a respectable man. Steady. A good head and stellar reputation. And I must say I've not seen you smile so readily in a very long time—nor witnessed such colour on your face."

"Father!"

"I only speak as any father should." He patted her hand, eyes still twinkling.

Belle shook her head. "Rafe merely helped me out with some paperwork. Besides, now that we've found what he's been looking for and once things get settled, I doubt he will be back on a daily basis . . . if at all."

Her father studied her for a moment, his expression softening. "And this troubles you."

Very much so!

But she couldn't say that.

She mustered a brave smile. "I have an orphanage to run, so I shall be busy anyway."

"Not if you take that offer."

She narrowed her eyes. "You just said I should not get 'tangled up' with Ben again."

"I did, and I stand by it." His voice grew firmer. "But that does not preclude the solicitors from carrying out the business for you. Tell you what, I shall check into the matter and find out why Haven House has become such a coveted prize for a man like Scrooge."

His offer lit a smile. "Would you, Father?"

"Of course." He squeezed her fingers. "That's what fathers are for."

Yet even as Belle thanked him, her thoughts drifted elsewhere—past the scheming of Scrooge and Marley, beyond even the uncertainty of what she should do about the offer—to a certain barrister and a bright-eyed boy whose absences might soon ache far more than any battle over Haven House.

Twelve

> It was a strange figure—like a child: yet not so like a child as like an old man, viewed through some supernatural medium.
>
> —Charles Dickens, *A Christmas Carol*

Two days later, Rafe pulled off his hat as he entered Haven House. It'd pained him sorely not to have visited yesterday, but after missing yet another important meeting in which Harvey had to cover for him, there had simply been no possible way to avoid being at the office. He should be there even now. But how could he stay away from his own nephew? As far as he was concerned, the sooner Cricket was brought home, the better—and a scourge to any naysayers who would deny the child such a comfort, even if it meant he might have to look for another job. It had been no easy decision to come by, and yet it was the only right one.

But he'd had precious little time to convince his mother of that.

"Miss Beaumont?" he called over the pounding of hammers ringing out from the main hall. A smirk twitched his lips at the all-too-familiar cacophony, for it felt like home. Thankfully, the renovations at his own house ought to be wrapped up by tonight. They'd better be! The Munro annual Christmas Open House was tomorrow evening.

He strode down the corridor to the playroom, making a mental note to remind his mother the committee needed to send over not only more teaching candidates but some prospective housemaids as well. Belle couldn't be expected to answer doors, mind children, oversee construction, and keep an eye on the dynamic Graybills.

"Miss Beaumont?" He stepped into a playroom that smelled of flour-paste. Only Tibby glanced up at him with a smile from where she sat in the middle of the rug amidst a blizzard of paper flakes. The rest of the children were far too preoccupied with snipping the life out of folded newsprint or painting glue on strips of paper. With small fists planted on her hips, Anne stood over Pippin, directing him like a general at war on the finer points of paper chain making. Jack wagged a finger at Rory, admonishing the youngling not to step on the drying snowflakes. Little Birdie swirled a finger around in the paste pot, then rubbed it on her cheek. No tired administrator was in sight. Nor was Cricket.

He scanned the far corners, gut clenching when he finally laid eyes on his nephew. Cricket sat cross-legged in a nook between bookshelf and window. Quiet. Separate. Folding and unfolding what looked to be a tattered attempt of a snowflake, a forgotten book on the floor next to him.

And his little shoulders bowed as if the weight of the world was his to uphold.

Bypassing the activity in the center of the room, Rafe approached the boy and crouched to his level. "Making something?"

Cricket nodded but did not look up.

Rafe waited.

"It's a snowflake," he mumbled. "But it keeps coming out wrong. Anne said so. Said if I were going to make such a mess of things, to keep out of the way." Finally, he looked up, his entire five-year-old heart in his eyes. "But I can't figure out what's wrong with it. Can you, sir?"

A lump the size of a Christmas pudding stuck in his throat, so Rafe merely held out his hand.

The child deposited the worn piece of paper, all wrinkled and torn, onto his palm. The original folds had been creased carefully, but now barely held the newsprint together. A fringe marked one side, made by too many timid cuts. Carefully, Rafe smoothed out the wrinkles, revealing exactly what Anne had said.

A mess.

"Is it wrong?" The barest hint of hope hung in Cricket's small voice.

"Not at all." Rafe smiled. "It's simply different."

The boy's face darkened. "Nobody wants ones that look funny. Nobody wants me either."

That stabbed. The words. The sentiment. The rejection that hung like a cloud over his sister's precious child. Rafe gritted his teeth, struggling to keep his emotions in check.

Ever so carefully, he turned the rumpled snowflake over in his hand. "You know"—he purposely kept his voice steady when everything in him wanted to lash out at the unfair pain this boy carried—"this little snowflake reminds me of a verse I read only this morning. Would you like to hear it?"

Cricket sucked in his lower lip, then ever so slowly, nodded.

"Psalm 147 says, 'He healeth the broken in heart, and bindeth up their wounds. He telleth the number of the stars; he calleth them all by their names.' Last time I looked at the night sky, I saw so many different stars I couldn't begin to describe them all. God made those stars. Each one different. Each one with a name. And not one of them is forgotten."

He held up the snowflake. "And I believe God smiles when He sees things like this too. Not because it's perfect, but because you made it. God made you as different from anyone else as this snowflake is from the other children's. And rest assured, my boy, that when He looks at you, He sees His own work, made with care, called by name, just like He made the stars."

Cricket's eyes widened. "You really think so?"

"I do." He tousled the boy's hair and rose, thighs cramped from squatting so long. "Now, I think this special snowflake would look the best right here in the window, where Miss Beaumont might think it was snowing—for she dearly wishes for snow." He looped one end of the paper around the window latch, then flattened the bottom portion of it against the glass. "There. What do you think?"

Cricket stood, staring up at the misfit flake. "I think . . ." His little shoulders straightened, and a smile curved his lips. "I shall name it Henry!"

"Excellent choice." Rafe grinned, then turned at the click of heels entering the room.

As soon as Belle spied him, she arched a brow. "Mr. Munro, I didn't realize you were here."

"And I didn't realize you were transforming the playroom into a paper mill." He tipped his head toward the children and their industry.

"Yes, well, I was hoping making decorations would keep them busy for the Graybills while I attend the reading of the will, only . . ." She sighed. "Well, you didn't happen to see Betty or Joe on your way here, did you?"

"Don't tell me you've lost them." He chuckled, half in jest, half in hoping the couple was well and truly gone for good.

"I'm afraid so, and when I need them most. Say"—she narrowed her eyes—"being that you are here, would you be able to stay awhile? I really cannot miss the appointment with Mr. Snably. I don't think it should take long, should it? You would know better than I, after all."

"A simple will reading could be finished in a quarter of an hour. A complicated one might take hours. And having experienced Mrs. Trumble's filing system, I suspect it will be anything but simple."

"Oh dear." She glanced at the door as if doing so would make the Graybills appear.

His mind immediately ticked through the list of tasks awaiting him at the office—depositions, witness statements, finishing the judge's request for a summary brief. All urgent. All crucial to keep the case from falling apart. If he had any hope of keeping

Ward Davis from transportation, he and Harvey needed every spare hour.

And yet . . .

Those beseeching eyes of hers. The exhaustion shadowed there. She needed help. And she'd asked him. Trusted him with the safekeeping of children she cared deeply about.

He blew out a long breath, the weight of his legal burdens shifting just enough for him to speak. "How about we make a deal? I'll stay here and tend the children as long as you attend the open house tomorrow evening." He held out his hand.

She shook it with a grin. "I believe we have a bargain, sir, that is, as long as the Graybills show up by then." She pulled away, more adorable than any woman had a right to be. "Oh, I forgot to ask how your mother took the news of, well . . ." Her gaze drifted to Cricket, still standing at the window and now speaking to Henry as if the snowflake were a bosom companion. "The matter of a certain child."

Thunder and turf! How to answer that? He couldn't very well tell the tenderhearted Isabelle Beaumont his mother outright refused to have anything to do with the boy.

But neither could he ignore her.

"She was . . ." Words stalled on his tongue.

Belle turned to him, curiosity in her gaze. "She was what?"

"Em, surprised. Naturally, she was *quite* surprised. But I think the idea of a child in the house has its appeal." Not for her, yet it wasn't a lie. He looked forward to Cricket's bright voice at home. But the conversation with his mother was too big of a snarl to untie in a room full of jabbering children with a woman who needed to be in a law office at the moment. "We can discuss this more at length later. You have a meeting to attend, and I have a paper chain to hang."

He turned to the children, but inside a quiet tension unfurled. He'd meant every word about the charm of a boy to brighten the silent house he shared with his mother. Yet ever since informing her of Cricket's existence, she'd fallen into a sorrowful stillness. No harsh words. No reproach. Not even any debate.

Only the aching quiet of a woman who mourned both what she'd lost and what she could not yet bear to fully face.

Slightly breathless and not just a little flustered, Belle finally arrived at the office of Drake, Meekum, and Clive. The coach she'd hired had gone the wrong way, adding a quarter of an hour travel time. Had it been snowing this morning—which it wasn't—she'd have been lucky to make it here on time. As it stood, the case clock was even now on the last chimes of ten o'clock.

Add to list: Next time hire a driver with a working sense of direction.

Behind a tall desk, a tightly buttoned clerk glanced up, his cravat so securely cinched, the fabric cut into his neck. "Ah, Miss Beaumont, I take it? Follow me, please."

He hopped off his stool and led her to an adjoining chamber. Inside, a modest fire crackled on the hearth, the scent of cherry tobacco and leather blending with the smoke. Two men she didn't recognize sat in front of a desk occupied by Mr. Snably. All rose at her entrance.

But where was her father?

Mr. Snably dipped his head, then offered her a chair front and center. "Please be seated, Miss Beaumont. My associates, Mr. Meekum and Mr. Drake, are here to witness the reading of Mrs. Trumble's will, and we are ready to begin."

"As you wish, but you should know my father—"

Just then the door opened, and in stepped the man himself. "My apologies, gentlemen, Belle. I hope I didn't keep you waiting."

"Not at all, Mr. Beaumont." Mr. Snably pulled over another chair. "We were just about to begin."

She exchanged a glance with her father as he sat next to her, noting the loose hair at his brow and rumpled frock coat. Apparently he'd had just as frenzied a morning as herself.

Behind the desk, Mr. Snably adjusted his spectacles. "We are gathered here today for the last will and testament of Mrs. Cordelia Trumble, dated the twenty-seventh of November, eighteen hundred nineteen. I shall now read aloud for the benefit of all parties present."

Belle's chest tightened at the mention of Mrs. Trumble's name. The dear woman had been so vividly alive, so much a part of Haven House it was nearly impossible to think she was well and truly gone. Yet now all that remained of her were sweet memories and the sound of her last wishes on the solicitor's tongue.

Clearing his throat, Mr. Snably lifted a crisp document. "To my few surviving relatives—Miss Eugenia Hennico of Puckeridge and Mr. Avery Merrell of Chipping Sodbury—both second cousins once removed on my mother's side, I leave the sum of one pound each, with the firm desire they shall use it to purchase something personally beneficial, such as some tooth powder or a new copy of the Holy Scriptures."

Belle's brows raised. Her father snorted.

"To my faithful, if occasionally misguided, caretakers," Mr. Snably continued, "Betty and Joe Graybill, I leave the sum of five pounds apiece and permission to continue residing at Haven House so long as they desire."

If they show up to claim it.

Belle held her fingers to her lips, hiding a smirk.

Add to list: Consider tethers for the Graybills or tasking a Bow Street runner to keep track of them.

"Now then." Mr. Snably sniffed. "To Isabelle Beaumont, I leave the entirety of Haven House—its buildings, furnishings, ledgers, debts, and duties—as well as the title of director. It is my belief that no one else possesses the grit, grace, or good sense to manage children of need."

The words struck deep, a bittersweet ache rising in Belle's chest. Mrs. Trumble's faith in her was humbling . . . and painfully final.

The solicitor looked up while setting the paper down. "Miss

Beaumont, you are now the legal owner and administrator of Haven House."

Well. That was it, then. Though she'd been managing the orphanage for nearly three weeks, save for the formality of the probate application, it was now official—which made it surprisingly hard to breathe all of a sudden. The responsibility of the house, the children, *everything*, all pressed in on her.

Oh, God, how can I do this?

Her father reached over and squeezed her hand, his strength a comfort, especially now.

Mr. Snably picked up a separate document. "There is also a final note regarding an outstanding offer of purchase currently still on file." Tucking his chin, he eyed her over the rim of his spectacles. "An offer for which a decision must soon be made."

Her father leaned forward. "About that, has there been any further correspondence on the matter? Any details as to what would happen to Haven House should my daughter decide to sell?"

The solicitor shook his head. "All I have is the standing offer of twelve thousand pounds. No further details were provided, and my inquiries—at Miss Beaumont's request—have gone unanswered. Mr. Scrooge has been most elusive."

"How very like the man," Belle murmured. Oh, when he'd first courted her, all had been sunshine and promises, but toward the end, when he'd begun to make something of his status, things changed. The last Christmas they'd shared, when he'd arrived for dinner, he'd come not with carols or cheer but with ledgers in his coat pocket and irritation in his dark eyes. He'd glanced more at the clock than at her. Her father had offered him a glass of port, but he'd declined, claiming time was money. When she handed him a small carved pipe box—one she'd saved weeks to buy—he barely looked at it before murmuring about frivolous customs and unnecessary expense. That was the night she stopped believing he loved her more than his ambitions.

Mr. Snably stacked the documents together and tapped them on the desktop, pulling her from the sour memory.

"If there are no further questions nor an answer to the offer . . ." He paused as if she might jump from the chair and say yes. "Then that concludes the reading. Copies of the will shall be available at the beginning of next week."

As they stood to leave, Belle turned to her father. "Thank you for coming."

"Of course." He pressed a kiss to her brow. "I wouldn't have missed it."

They stepped into the receiving hall, her quick step outpacing her father's as he lingered to chat with Mr. Snably. She couldn't afford such a luxury. Even now Rafe should be on his way to work instead of minding the children for her. She could only hope the Graybills had returned from wherever they'd disappeared to. And if they hadn't, how would she manage with only her and Mrs. Bakewell in a house full of rambunctious orphans?

She squared her shoulders as she reached for the front door latch. She would have to manage. Somehow. After all, she was the director now—a position that was proving much harder than she expected.

But truly, how much worse could it get?

THIRTEEN

> He was conscious of a thousand odours floating in the air, each one connected with a thousand thoughts, and hopes, and joys, and cares long, long, forgotten!
>
> —Charles Dickens, *A Christmas Carol*

Either this was Belle's most brilliant idea—or her worst. But those words of Rafe's two days ago—*"I think the idea of a child in the house has its appeal"*—had sounded so winsome at the time that they'd stuck with her. And there'd been something wistful in his voice as well. Something she suspected he hadn't meant to let slip. A yearning, perhaps? A desire for the joy only a child could bring? Or maybe for something other than the barrister's stuffy world of courtrooms and case files? She blew a low breath into the frosty night air as she stood on the stoop of the Munro town house. Brilliant or not, here she was, Cricket's mittened hand clinging tightly to hers.

Bundled in his woolen coat with cheeks rosy from the cold, the boy held up a wrinkled snowflake garland she'd helped him make earlier that day. Thankfully the Graybills had returned after their unexplained absence, and to be truthful, she wished they hadn't explained where they'd been. Something about searching for a lost boot that had managed to turn into a romp through Limehouse.

"Do you really think he'll like it?" Cricket's small voice, while warbly, held a heart full of hope.

"Mr. Munro shall love it." She smiled. And he would. She had no doubt about that.

Still, she hesitated on the stoop. The Christmas Open House was hardly a children's affair. It was more a parade of benefactors and charitable ladies exchanging polite flattery over steaming cups of posset.

But it was a little late for that now.

So she rang the bell, the buzz of the inside partygoers leaching into the night through the merrily lit windows.

Moments later, the door opened, and a footman in midnight-blue livery glanced from her to the boy, one of his brows arching ever so slightly. "May I help you, madam?"

She handed over the invitation Rafe had given her.

After a cursory glance, he ushered them in and helped them out of their coats, then directed them through a lavish front hall into a world of crystal chandeliers and flocked papered walls. The heels of her shoes sank into a carpet so plush it seemed to swallow her steps. Gilded cornices gleamed against a lily-white plastered ceiling, and everything smelled of wealth—of rose attar and polished wood, silk upholstery and lavender-scented candlewax. The ladies shimmered in their satin gowns, and the gents were dressed to the nines in their bespoke suits. Cricket's little jaw dropped.

Her mouth pinched. This was too much. The opulence of just this one room instantly put her on edge. This was the sort of living Ben had longed for—had slaved for—at the expense of their relationship. Was that the sort of man Rafe was too? Her heart wanted to believe he was different—that the barrister with the boyish grin and direct stare didn't care a fig for the charms of this world . . . but what if he did? What if beneath his warmth was another tortured soul who prized appearances over people?

God, please don't let that be so! Not again.

She smoothed a hand down her skirts and forced a smile for Cricket. This was no time for doubts, but they hung there all the same, rustling in the corner of her mind like dead leaves caught in an eddy.

"And who might this young gentleman be?" A beak-nosed matron in a sunshine-yellow gown swooped over and held a lorgnette to her eye, smiling at Cricket.

"Ooh!" Another lady with the same distinctive nose practically squealed as she bent to his level and pinched his cheek. "I daresay you are the most dapper man here this evening."

To his credit, the boy didn't shy away. He bowed just as Belle had taught him for an occasion such as this. "My name's Cricket. Pleased to meet your acquaintance. And this here is Miss Beaumont." He looked up at her, questions in his eyes.

"Well done," she whispered to him, then spoke louder to the ladies as she dipped them a curtsey. "Good evening."

The woman in the yellow dress nodded her greeting. "That is quite an escort you have with you tonight, Miss Beaumont. I daresay Mrs. Munro will be quite in raptures to meet this young fellow."

"Indeed," the other lady chimed in. "If I had a bonnet feather for every heart he's sure to win tonight, I daresay it would look as if a peacock had nested on my head." A shrill laugh followed by a snort from the woman turned Rafe's head from across the room.

And a handsome smile lit his face. He wove his way through the merrymakers to her side. "I see you've met Mrs. Beesome and her sister, longtime friends of—" His eyes locked on Cricket, confusion furrowing his brow slightly. "Ah, Master Cricket. I didn't realize you would be joining us tonight."

"Miss Beaumont said you might not mind if I came too . . . just for a little while. And I made this specially for you, sir." He held up the wrinkled snowflake garland.

Belle leaned close to Rafe as he collected the offering, speaking for him alone. "I hope you don't mind. Being that you weren't able to stop over today, I thought you might like to see the boy."

Before he could answer, Cricket bounced on his toes. "This

is my first party, sir. I've never seen so many fancy people all at once."

Mrs. Beesome and her sister tittered. "Oh! He is too adorable. Such a charmer!"

Behind Rafe, a woman approached, garbed in elegant green velvet with garnet-drop earbobs. Silver threaded what was once lush raven tresses, and her eyes were the same stormy blue as Rafe's. Her cheekbones and the way she arched a brow mimicked him as well. His mother, most likely.

"What is all this delight I hear from across the room?" Her gaze drifted down to Cricket. "And who is this little gentleman stealing the hearts of half my guests?"

"My name's Cricket, mum." Once again he bowed, then grabbed Belle's hand, his little palm sweaty against hers. "Miss Beaumont brought me. She and Mr. Munro are friends."

"Are they?" A spark of interest lit Mrs. Munro's expression as she glanced between Rafe and her. The corners of her mouth curved slightly—as if she'd been waiting for this.

Rafe cleared his throat. "Forgive me for not making proper introductions. Miss Beaumont, please meet my mother, Mrs. Rosamund Munro. Mother, this is Miss Isabelle Beaumont, director of Haven House."

Her eyes brightened. "Ah! The lady who keeps my son so busy these days. Well, I can see why." She smiled at Belle before turning back to Cricket. "And you, young sir, what mischief do you bring with you tonight?"

Cricket grinned. "Miss Beaumont said I could come along if I promised to be good. And I brought Mr. Munro some Christmas cheer—that's what she calls it." He pointed at the garland in Rafe's hand.

"Charming!" Mrs. Munro's voice softened, almost wistful as she studied the boy. "Why, you have the same eyes and tilt of head as my—"

She stopped, the colour draining from her face.

And Belle felt the shift immediately, the warmth in the room thinning like breath on glass.

Rafe's mother straightened, composure resettling on her features. "Haven House, you said?"

"Yes," Belle said carefully.

A pause—long enough to see a flicker of longing in the woman's eyes as she peeked once more at Cricket. "How good of you to bring him, though . . ." Her jaw tightened. "I confess I wasn't expecting children this evening. Such gatherings can be overwhelming."

Belle slipped an arm around the lad's shoulders. "Cricket is quite used to lively rooms, ma'am."

Mrs. Beesome clapped her hands. "What a delightful lad!"

"Indeed," Mrs. Munro murmured. "Well, if you will all excuse me, I must speak with the kitchen staff. I cannot have the punch growing tepid."

She turned away, the thick green velvet of her skirt swaying as she crossed the room.

Tepid punch? Not likely. Belle's stomach knotted. Leaning close to Rafe, she whispered, "I hope I haven't made a mistake in bringing Cricket here."

A muscle on the side of his neck jumped. "Neither you nor Cricket is at fault. Please excuse me for a moment."

He vanished into the crowd just like his mother.

Belle frowned.

Add to list: Never again make such an impetuous decision—or walk blind into someone else's storm.

Rafe hurried after his mother, weaving through the corridor, uneasy at how suddenly she had fled the room. He could only hope Cricket hadn't sensed the change in her. And Belle . . . well, that would be another conversation entirely.

"Mother," he called after her, "I would have a word with you."

She didn't answer, only gathered her skirts and quickened her step.

He frowned. This wasn't anger. It was something else. Something raw she did not wish him to see.

But so be it.

He caught up and, with gentle insistence, touched her arm, drawing her aside into the shelter of a window alcove.

"Rafe Julius Munro!" A censure, but one more startled than affronted. "I am your mother. Do not corner me so rudely."

"I mean no disrespect." He searched her face, gentling his tone. "But you left the room as if Miss Beaumont and the boy had committed a crime simply by being there."

Her lips parted, then pressed together again. After a beat, she shook her head slightly. "I was not prepared to see him . . . to see your sister's face in his. It—it felt like losing her twice."

"Then don't turn away from him. He is all that remains of her."

"You don't understand." Grief tightened her mouth. "I cannot betray her wishes."

He reached for her hands, helpless against the powerful sorrow so obvious on her face.

She pulled back at his touch. "Please—" Her voice cracked. "I have no strength for this tonight."

Her skirts whispered as she moved away, leaving him alone in the corridor. How could love ache so keenly on both sides of a secret?

Oh, Mother.

He scrubbed a hand over his face, then let it fall with a sigh that felt too big to hold. How could she see that boy and still turn away? Apparently there'd be no swaying her to Cricket's side. Not tonight, anyway.

But this wasn't over.

And Belle—

Oh, sweet mercy. He'd left her quite hastily.

He strode to the front of the house, heart hammering with more than frustration. He had to fix what could still be mended.

He scanned the partygoers, but neither she nor the boy were

in sight. Mrs. Beesome was, though. Her yellow gown stood out like the blazing sun on a stormy day.

Weaving his way through the merrymakers, he approached the two sisters near the punch table. "Pardon me, Mrs. Beesome, but have you seen where Miss Beaumont and Cricket have gone?"

"Oh yes." She saluted him with her glass. "They made quite an elegant farewell, begging off for the sake of the child. Past his bedtime, you know."

"Thank you." He fled to the front door, not even bothering to grab his coat and hat as he darted into the night. Outside, two houses down, a hackney door shut, and the jarvey clicked his tongue with a loud "Walk on!"

Rafe took off at a dead run, the chill December air knifing through his waistcoat. Hopefully that coach contained Belle and the boy, but just to be certain, he bellowed at the driver. "Ho, there! Are you carrying a lady and a boy?"

The jarvey barely glanced back. "Aye, but I don't see how that is any business of yours, sir." The man cracked the reins, and the hackney surged forward.

So did Rafe.

He sprinted the last few strides, then launched himself upward. His foot struck the narrow step just as his hand latched on to the side rail. A jolt rattled up his arm, but he swung himself onto the moving coach like a man possessed and yanked the door open.

The coach jerked to a halt.

"Off with ye, ye thieven' cully!" The jarvey thwacked the side of the coach with his whip. "The lady ain't paid fer no—"

Rafe flipped the man a shilling.

Which promptly shut him up.

"Whoa!" Cricket cried from inside. "You hopped up here like a highwayman! Wait till I tell Jack!"

Rafe grinned as he stepped fully into the coach and took the seat opposite the boy and Belle. He pulled the door shut behind him, and the wheels once again rattled against the cobbles.

Belle scrunched her brow, the scant lamplight of the coach torches bathing her face, making her look impossibly lovely. "What are you doing here? You have a party to attend. Guests to entertain."

He shook his head. "This is more important."

"*We're* more important than a party?" Cricket bounced on his seat.

Rafe chuckled. "Yes, you are."

For a few breaths, only the questions in Belle's eyes spoke. Questions he wasn't sure how to answer with an overeager boy listening to every word.

"Miss Beaumont, I . . ." He shifted uncomfortably on the worn leather bench, the scent of cigar smoke and sausage worn into the fabric. "Well, I wanted to say I am glad you and Cricket came to the party."

She angled her head. "You are?"

"Very much so. I didn't want you to leave without knowing that. You two are much too important to let any misunderstandings come between us, and it would be my honour to escort you home. That is, if you will allow me?"

"Pah!" Cricked waved his hand in the air. "'Course we do."

Despite the boy's enthusiasm, Rafe held Belle's gaze. He'd not force his company on her if she did not wish it.

A slow smile curved her lips. "I suppose it would be dangerous to deny a highwayman his request."

Grasping the seat as the coach rounded a corner, Cricket leaned forward, eyes wide. "Are you really a highwayman, sir?"

Rafe laughed outright at that. "Only the kind that steals moments, not purses."

Belle studied him through her lashes. "I . . . I hope all is well between you and your mother. I pray I didn't cause any undue strife."

He tugged on his sleeve cuffs, schooling his tone to nonchalance. "My mother has wrestled with grief for a long time. It is always two steps forward, one back." He shrugged. "Tonight was just part of the pattern. Do not blame yourself."

"I don't. Not for her grief, leastwise. As for my impetuousness, however—"

He held up a finger, cutting her off. "I prefer to think of it as spontaneity, and you saw how Mrs. Beesome and her sister were delighted because of it. Why, I daresay you made their evening. They'll be enraptured by the boy's charm for the next week and a half."

"You think so?"

"I know so. Besides, sometimes a storm is just what's needed to wash away the dirt of the past."

She didn't answer. Just held his gaze with such intensity it rooted him to the spot. So many words unsaid, hanging between them like mist.

Cricket, oblivious, yawned loudly. "Miss Beaumont says storms make the air cleaner, but I don't know about dirt."

That broke the tension, and he glanced at the boy with fondness curling in his chest.

The cab juddered to a stop. Belle reached for the door. Rafe beat her to it, pressing his hand to the latch.

"Thank you for coming after us," she said softly. "For making me—and Cricket—a priority."

He leaned close as he opened the door. "I wasn't about to let the two brightest parts of my night vanish into the dark without a proper good-bye."

Her cheeks pinked, and her eyes flicked to his mouth. And no wonder. One little shift—just one—and he could close the space between them. Take the risk.

And ruin everything.

He hopped down and offered her a hand. She placed her gloved fingers in his, and for a moment, the world fell away—

Until Cricket flew out the door like a cannonball.

"Cricket!" Belle cried.

Rafe caught the boy midair with a laugh. "Good night, young master," he said as he set the boy down.

"Good night, sir!" Cricket chirped as he yanked open the front gate and tore down the path to the front door of Haven House.

Rafe turned back to Belle, suddenly alone with her. Solemnly, he offered his arm, not out of formality but out of something far more tender and deliberate. "May I walk you to the door?"

After a breath of hesitation, she placed her hand lightly in the crook of his elbow.

They walked in companionable silence, the soft crunch of pea gravel the only sound.

At the door, he paused, unwilling to leave her quite yet. He couldn't. The soft glow of the door lanterns painted her face like a masterpiece.

"You are braver than I realized," he said quietly. "And more generous than most people deserve."

"And you are not the man I expected."

"No?" He tilted his head.

"You are better," she breathed.

His heart kicked against his ribs. Before he knew it, he'd lifted her hand and pressed his lips against the back of her glove, feeling the heat beneath. Craving more than a piece of fabric against his mouth.

He released her before he could act on the temptation to yank off the glove and pull her into his arms. "Good night, Belle."

"Good night, Rafe. Oh! I nearly forgot. Tomorrow afternoon I am taking the children caroling. We could use a baritone, if you're free, that is."

He wasn't. Not really. There was only Saturday and Sunday before the Grindlethorn trial on Monday. He should be buried in statements and strategies. But if he drank excessively dark tea and put off sleep, then . . . perhaps?

He nodded, already committed. "Name the time."

She smiled, luminous. "Four o'clock. See you then."

He waited until she disappeared inside Haven House, then forced himself to turn away. As he walked down the lane, the warmth of her presence faded all too quickly, and he was overtaken by a chill that had nothing to do with the December air. His mother's words returned to him again, thin and fractured.

"Please—I have no strength for this tonight."

Rafe exhaled slowly, his chest tightening. It wasn't so much refusal that he'd heard in her voice but exhaustion. Grief stretched too thin. Cricket wasn't merely a complication to her, but a living reminder of everything she'd buried with her daughter. What if this situation broke something inside his mother that had already once been mended?

FOURTEEN

"There was a boy singing a Christmas Carol at my door last night. I should like to have given him something; that's all."

—Charles Dickens, *A Christmas Carol*

Rafe held on to his hat as he wound through the pedestrians clogging the London streets on this late Saturday afternoon. Some held packages. Others held hands. All in all, it was quite the obstacle course, but he'd made a promise to Belle, and he would keep it even if it meant leaping over a cart of roasted chestnuts—which he hadn't done yet—or practically dancing while trying to sidestep a meat seller holding aloft a flailing goose—which he had.

As he rounded the corner onto Candlewick Street, a rather squawking rendition of "God Rest Ye Merry, Gentlemen" rose above the clatter of coach wheels. The closer he drew to the sound, the more clearly he could pick out Belle's sweet soprano trying to guide the children back to a purer refrain.

And then he spied them. Seven children sang with their mouths open wide, their cheeks rosy-nipped from the December cold and their necks wrapped snugly in knit mufflers of various colours. Belle stood poised directly behind them, grasping the mittened hands of Rory and little Birdie. She was a beacon in the gathering shadows of evening, her smile steady despite the yowling harmony of young voices.

He snuck up alongside her—or tried to. Somehow Cricket always seemed to know when he was around. The lad broke rank and grabbed his hand, giving it a good swing. "You came!"

He stooped to the boy's ear and whispered, "I did, but it is time for singing, young master, not talking."

With that, Rafe straightened and joined in on the final chorus, Belle's appreciative grin warming a spot deep in his chest.

When the song ended, Jack kicked a cobblestone with his toe, a scowl creasing his brow. "I'm hungry. Can we go home now?"

"Not yet." Belle wagged a finger at him. "How about 'Joy to the World,' children?"

The words weren't even out of her mouth before Tibby and Pippin burst into song, and soon the rest joined in. Shoppers smiled at the group. One even pressed a coin into Anne's fingers.

Belle leaned close to Rafe, speaking low as the children sang. "I was beginning to think you weren't going to make it."

He angled his face toward her, their cheeks nearly touching. As it was, the mist of their breath mingled together in the space between. "Miss caroling with you? Never. Though I admit I was nearly bested by a goose just to get here."

She laughed lightly. "I would've loved to have seen that."

Not as much as I love seeing you.

He clamped his mouth shut lest the words escape. Is this what he'd become in a matter of only three weeks? Some sort of lovelorn schoolboy?

Pull yourself together, man!

She gazed at him through lowered lashes, her eyes catching the glow of a recently lit streetlamp. "Well, I'm glad you're here. The children seem to sing twice as loud when you're beside them."

"Is that so?" he murmured. "Then I shall have to stand here the rest of the evening."

Her smile softened into something quieter, something that tugged at the center of his chest. "I wouldn't mind that at all."

He should step back now. Should look away. But instead—fool that he was—he gave in to losing himself in the rich brown of her eyes and scent of cinnamon on her skin.

Until little Birdie squirmed between them, and Cricket tugged on his hand. "Hey! You're not singing, sir! And this is the best part."

Rafe chuckled as he stepped back to break the heady feel of standing so close to Belle, but not far enough to lose the enchantment entirely. *Duty calls*, he mouthed to Belle, then joined in with a hearty, "'And heaven and nature sing!'"

"The Holly and the Ivy" followed. Birdie decided she'd rather hold Anne's hand, and Rory—declaring he was big enough to stand on his own—pushed his way to stand by Jack. After that, they began a rousing rendition of "Hark! The Herald Angels Sing," but halfway through it, the bark of a man spoilt the chorus.

"What a load of humbug! Clogging up the streets like this, caterwauling like a bunch of bagged cats. It's a crime, I tell you! Where's a watchman when you need one? Get out of my way!"

Rafe turned his head at the complaint just as an "Oomph!" spilled out of Belle, and she toppled sideways. He barely caught her before she hit the cobblestones. He righted her—admittedly enjoying the feel of her in his arms—then glowered at the man who'd so rudely bumped into her. He was a sharp fellow, nose as pointed as a quill, dark eyes cutting in their malice. His mouth pinched as if a needle had sown his lips into puckers, and his step cut a swath right through the children.

Outrage fisted in Rafe's gut. That face. He knew it. The miser. The shark. Jacob Marley was a scourge across three boroughs and then some. The snappish man stomped past them without so much as a backward glance, his threadbare coat flapping like a warning. How dare he!

Rafe struck out after the bully—only to be pulled back by a tug on his sleeve and a "Rafe, don't" from Belle.

He glanced at her, the simmering urge to give the man the comeuppance he deserved cooling by degrees in light of Belle's beseeching gaze. "Let him go. I am fine, as are the children."

True. The incident had done nothing to stop their Christmas crooning. Cricket even grinned up at him—and it was only then he noticed the boy was missing a tooth.

"What's this?" Crouching, he tipped the child's face up, thoughts of the boorish Mr. Marley fading. "Why, you've lost a tooth, my good man."

Cricket giggled. "I'm not a man. Not yet. Jack says I'm naught but a guppy who can't even swim." His face twisted. "Not sure what that means, though."

Rafe gritted his teeth. He was going to have to talk with Jack about his insolent tongue lest the boy end up growing into the likes of Jacob Marley. For now, though, Rafe pulled a coin from his pocket and tucked it into Cricket's mitten. "Some say it's good luck to give a coin for a lost tooth. Just don't spend it all on sweets, hmm?"

The boy's eyes widened. "No, sir! I would never—"

"Rafe! There you are, at last! It was no small thing to get your location out of those two muddleheaded servants at Haven House."

Charles Harvey's bellow turned Rafe around, his breath immediately tight. What the deuce was his law partner doing here on Candlewick? "Harvey? I told you I'd be back by six. Why hunt me down here?"

"There's been a . . . well, let's call it an upset, for the sake of the woman and children." He nodded at Belle and her crew. "You'd better come, Munro. Immediately."

Rafe's brows drew into a line of steel.

This couldn't be good.

Hesitation, concern, maybe even a smidgeon of fear played over Rafe's face. The faint glow of the streetlamp caught in his eyes, turning them near-silver, and Belle's stomach sank. As much as she longed to keep him beside her—to hold tight to the warmth he brought simply by standing next to her—he had duties that far outweighed singing on a corner with her clutch of ragamuffins. She rested her gloved hand on the wool of his coat sleeve, touching so lightly it barely stirred the fabric. "Go on, Rafe. We've only a few more songs, and I daresay I've braved worse than a frosty evening without a baritone."

He looked at her then, admiration shining in his storm-blue gaze. "You are remarkable," he murmured, a tenderness in his voice she had no right to feel so giddy about—but she did. "Thank you," he added, and then he strode away with Mr. Harvey.

The instant he disappeared around the corner, the charm of Christmas caroling broke like thin ice beneath a heavy boot. The next verse faltered. The harmony splintered. The brisk cold, which hadn't bothered her before, crept under her pelisse and shivered up her spine.

And there was still no snow.

But she would not be so easily vanquished!

Add to list: Stock up on emotional fortitude and wear an added woolen skirt when popping around town.

Cricket still beamed, singing loudly, but Jack hovered at the far edge of the group, arms crossed, lips pulled into a sulk instead of proclaiming holiday cheer.

She pulled him closer with a light tug on his arm. "Come on, Jack. It's our last song, and you have the loudest voice of us all."

He wrenched away. "Tell your precious little pet there he can sing louder." He hitched a thumb at Cricket, who'd grabbed her hand and was swinging it carefree. "Cricket always gets special attention, like he's some lord's lost son."

"That's enough," Belle said firmly.

But Jack narrowed his eyes at Cricket, mouth twisting. "But even if you are, bet that lord wouldn't want you. Your own mum didn't want you. That's why you're here. Nobody wants you, little guppy."

"I said that's enough!" Her voice cracked like a whip, turning the heads of all the children and effectively ending the caroling.

Cricket froze, the swing of his arm going limp, then ever so slowly, his small fingers slipped from her grasp like melting snow.

She turned on the bigger boy. "Jack, you will apologize this instant."

His chin hardened, making it a miracle the tight "I'm sorry" could eke out between such flattened lips.

Cricket nodded, saying nothing, practically curling in on himself to block the cruelty of the world. No five-year-old should be so practiced at shutting out pain.

"I think we are finished caroling for today, children. Everyone back to Haven House." She reached for Cricket's hand, but he merely started trudging ahead. There were a few groans and some dragging feet, but no one argued. Thankfully. Little Birdie yawned, so she scooped up the two-year-old and steered Rory with a grasp of his collar.

By the time they reached the orphanage gate, her fingers were stiff with cold. She fumbled with the key, distracted by Cricket's silence and Jack's now-perpetual scowl. Perhaps he really was hungry and a bowl of stew would set him to rights. Betty could read books after supper, and Joe could pop some corn. Hopefully that would salvage the evening.

She opened the front door.

Then stopped short.

Joe Graybill stood in the hall with a satchel slung over one shoulder. Beside him, Betty clutched her handbag with both hands, her mouth flattened to a grim line.

"We're leaving," Joe said without preamble.

So much for popcorn and stories.

"But it is time for supper." Belle unbuttoned little Birdie's coat as the other children filed past her, already tugging off mufflers and mittens. "Where are you going?"

Joe aimed a finger at the deconstructed front room. "We found a mouse nest in the ashes."

Betty's face turned grave. "And a spent coal too. Like the little blighters were trying to finish off what the last fire didn't do."

Joe nodded solemnly. "They've gone from scurrying to scheming. Last night, I swear one stared me down. Just sat on the windowsill, twitching 'is little nose at me. Bold as you please."

Belle blinked as she hung up little Birdie's coat, and the child scampered off. "I haven't seen a mouse recently, so I don't really know what you're talking about."

Betty wagged her head as if Belle were the simpleton. "That's the problem, miss. Those furry bandits like you. You and the children—singing and traipsing about, leaving crumbs in your wake. O' course they wouldn't threaten you."

"It's us what they're after," Joe added. "And I won't stand for it. My wife and I are not waiting for whiskers in our bedding or our eyebrows to be singed off in the night."

Belle just stared, for what was there to say to that absurdity?

"We're off to my sister's in Hampstead. When—and if—you rid this place of those horrid creatures, we may consider returning. Until then, best o' luck to ye." Betty hooked her arm through Joe's. "Good-bye."

"But—"

"Good-bye, miss," Joe echoed as he led his wife past her and out into the night.

The door clicked shut behind them.

Down the hall, a squabble rang out from the playroom—something about who would sit nearest the hearth.

For a long while, Belle stood rooted to the floorboards, stunned by the abruptness of it all. Just like that, the Graybills were gone. It was only her now. Her and Mrs. Bakewell. Left to manage seven rambunctious children . . . and possibly a legion of invisible, vengeful mice with a taste for ash and arson.

Her shoulders slumped. Father had been right to question whether she could shoulder this responsibility.

She unpinned her hat with shaking fingers. "Right, then," she whispered, squaring her shoulders.

But tears burned her eyes. Bravado, no matter how finely playacted, didn't make her capable. Perhaps the kindest thing she could do for the children was to admit defeat. And being that her father had found nothing untoward in Ben's offer thus far . . . well.

She was now of a mind to take it.

Fifteen

"Merciful Heaven, what is this!"
—Charles Dickens, *A Christmas Carol*

Judge Flintwick had never been a favorite of Rafe's—and this morning, the big-bellied man slipped even further from his favor. Rafe had hardly set down his red bag and smoothed the first sheet of notes when the judge began drumming his fingers—loudly—on the bench, his eyes flicking to the clock with thinly veiled impatience.

Honestly, it had all started unraveling two days prior, when Harvey had yanked Rafe away from the caroling festivities with the promise of something urgent—an upset, or so he'd claimed. Rafe had hoped it might be the break they needed, a new key witness or the like, something that could shake the foundation of the Crown's case.

But the upset, as it turned out, was Mrs. Hammer's new "memory."

She now claimed she'd not only seen Ward Davis leaving Grindlethorn's property, but that he had blood on his sleeve—a detail she hadn't mentioned in any of her previous statements. A bit convenient, that. Too convenient. As if someone had fed it to her.

And now, barely an hour into the trial, Rafe knew without

doubt there was nothing fair about this fight for justice. Flintwick had a mission, and Rafe suspected it had everything to do with the man clearing his schedule by lunch. After all, there was no time for a thorough hearing when roast mutton was on the line.

So now, as Mrs. Hammer repeated her testimony, Rafe sat rigid at the defense table, hands clenched in his lap, praying the jurors would see her for who she was—a nearsighted busybody who'd sell her own mother's molars for a coin or two.

Harvey stood a few paces before the witness box, one hand tucked behind his back, the other gesturing smoothly as he posed the questions he and Rafe had crafted over the weekend. His tone was calm, almost bored—until he produced the small letterboard used in courtrooms for demonstrating vision and asked Mrs. Hammer to read the second line. She squinted, leaned forward . . .

And still got it wrong.

Rafe's gaze darted to the jurors, eager to witness a spark of suspicion about the woman's testimony. But no. Not even a blink. One juror yawned. Another picked at his cuff.

And Judge Flintwick interrupted Harvey. "Move it along," he said. "This is not the time for an eye examination."

Rafe risked a glance at Ward Davis, standing in the dock. A cornered animal couldn't look more wary. His fingers clutched the rail as if holding it kept him from falling into an abyss. His face was ashen, his jaw clenched so tight that the muscles ticked in his cheek. His eyes darted from jury to judge to him, quiet, pleading . . .

Desperate.

Rafe's gut clenched. The man already looked half bound, as if invisible chains were wrapping around him. Harvey dropped into his chair at the defense table, muttering an oath under his breath. This was not going well.

Not well at all.

Stiffening, Rafe pulled out his closing remarks for a quick review.

"Come, come, Mr. Munro." Flintwick gestured with a swipe of his arm, his black robe swinging in the air like a scythe. "We've not got all day, unless you choose to waive your closing remarks to the jury?" Without waiting for an answer, he lifted the gavel. "That being said, I make a move to—"

Rafe stood at once. "Pardon me, sir, but I should very much like to present a final appeal to reason—with your leave, of course."

The judge's thick lips curved downward, his gavel moving ever so slowly back to its cradle. "Fine, Mr. Munro, but make it quick."

Praying for mercy, Rafe approached the twelve men, sweating beneath his black robes despite the chill in the courtroom.

"Gentlemen of the jury," he began, ignoring the perspiration on his neck and the itch of the woolen wig atop his head, "on August seventh, London believed it witnessed a murder, yet there was no blood save for the mention from Mrs. Hammer. There was no confession. Most importantly of all, there was no motive worthy of this crime in relation to Mr. Ward Davis. All we have is the word of a woman whose eyesight is—"

"Ahem." Flintwick gave a theatrical cough, tapping his gavel once, sharply. "Spare us the editorial, Mr. Munro. Bare facts are all that is needed."

"Yes, Your Honour." Rafe swallowed back what he really wanted to say. Not only was it unfair of the judge to interrupt him, it was downright unethical. Suppressing a scowl, he met each juror's gaze as he paced in front of them. "I ask only that you consider how difficult it is to see the truth from a distance—especially when one wants so badly to believe what they think they saw."

Flintwick tapped the gavel again. "Wrap it up, counsel. You are beating a dead horse."

Rafe gritted his teeth. Time for a different tack. "Ward Davis stands before you not as a villain, but as a son, a tradesman, a young man trying to make his way. He is guilty of nothing more than poverty and proximity. Today you are being asked not to weigh a confession. You are being asked to guess. If we convict a man on suspicion and flimsy circumstantial evidence, then none of us is safe. And so, I submit that you, gentlemen, are not merely deciding this case. You are setting precedent for how we treat the voiceless, the powerless, the poor. In light of that, let your verdict be one that history will be proud to echo. Do the right thing, men. That is all anyone can ask."

The instant he dipped his head at the judge, signaling the end of his speech, Flintwick sped through jury instructions, and the men filed out with a bailiff in the lead.

Rafe took his seat next to Harvey, leaning aside to ask in a whisper if there was anything he might've missed, but before his partner could answer, the jury shuffled back into the courtroom.

Rafe's heart stopped beating.

This was either the best possible outcome . . . or the worst. All sat save for the foreman.

Judge Flintwick, robes rustling, cleared his throat. "I commend you for a speedy response, my good men, and so I ask, members of the jury, have you reached a verdict?"

Rafe held his breath. No doubt Davis did as well, but he'd not glance at him. He couldn't. His eyes were fixed on the foreman's mouth, waiting for an answer. Hoping for justice.

Frantic for a miracle.

"We have, Your Honour," the foreman replied. "It is our unanimous consensus that we find the defendant, Mr. Ward Davis, guilty of the murder of Mr. Thomas Grindlethorn."

Rafe closed his eyes, the sharp gasp from Davis stabbing him square in the chest. No. No! This could not be happening.

The judge—practically gleeful—ran through the sentence at top speed. Transportation to the penal colonies in Australia. Hard labour. No possible return to England.

Behind him in the spectators, a lady howled, then swooned. Davis's mother. The moment the gavel banged for the final time, the courtroom erupted in a low murmur. Rafe exchanged a glance with Harvey, and they both approached Davis before the poor soul was hauled off.

"Don't despair." Rafe squeezed the man's arm, despising the shackles on the young fellow's thin wrists. "This was a setback, but we shall appeal. Do you understand?"

Davis's mouth contorted, but he said nothing. Two bailiffs led him away. Rafe watched him go, a gaping pit opening wide in his chest.

He'd failed.

Just like before.

He'd ruined a man's life.

Nay. He'd lost it.

Harvey cuffed him on the back. "Take heart, Munro. We did the best we could."

Rafe raked a hand through his hair, suspecting that had he not spent so much time at Haven House, he maybe could have done better. He gave a sad shake of his head. "It wasn't enough."

Harvey blew a huge puff of air. "Defeat never comes easily, I'm afraid."

"It was my fault," Rafe whispered.

But Harvey didn't hear, not with a bailiff calling for the room to clear. Rafe gathered his papers mechanically, his throat raw from all the arguments he'd given to deaf ears. He begged off Harvey's invitation to join him at the Boar's Head for a lobster and lettuce, his appetite devoured by shame.

In the robing room, he stripped off his gown and wig, folding them as reverently as a mourner caring for the clothes of the dead. He set them on the shelf, then just stood there, staring. He had come into this case with conviction and purpose. Rafe Munro, the mighty junior barrister. Champion of the downtrodden. And now? A bitter laugh stuck in his throat like a fishbone. Now a man would be shipped halfway around the world, branded a killer, because Rafe hadn't been clever enough to stop it.

With nothing but his red bag and a soul full of sorrow, he made his way outside. Damp cold wrapped around him like judgment. He hailed a hackney, but even as one approached, he wasn't sure where he would go. Belle's face flashed in his mind, the only thing soft and warm about this wretched day. Oh, how he longed for her comfort, for the way she might reach for his hand in companionship or tilt her head not with pity but pure empathy.

Yet he had no right to burden her with this.

Nor did he wish for her to see the failure of the counsel who couldn't protect the innocent—the one who'd let a young man be led off to his probable death.

With a shudder, Rafe hopped into the coach, the chains of Ward Davis echoing in his ears like a sentence he couldn't unhear.

Like the guilt he'd carry the rest of his life.

Belle brushed a stray lock of hair from her sweaty forehead, the coarse towels warm against her chilled fingers. The damp scent of lye clung to the fabric from the early morning wash. Mrs. Bakewell had hired a laundry girl—one who refused to fold linens. Just one more trouble atop a growing pile of misfortune.

Sighing, Belle strode down the corridor leading to the front of Haven House. It'd been two days since the Graybills' desertion. Two days of Cricket's head hanging and nothing but mumbles when addressed. He hadn't even picked up a book. The search for mice had proven fruitless. Mrs. Bakewell was voicing mutiny. So was the construction foreman—for he claimed the old walls were riddled with crumbled mortar, and he threatened to quit if she didn't agree to let him tear out more than half the front room. Which of course wouldn't do. Not with Christmas in less than a week. And still not a single snowflake had fallen from the leaden clouds hanging over London like a fist.

Her shoulders slumped as she shifted the load of towels into one arm so she could grab the balustrade. A tumble down the stairs and a broken ankle would only add to her difficulties. Hopefully Rafe was faring better than her with his court case.

She prayed it was going well because she wasn't sure she could handle one more disaster, even one that didn't directly affect her.

She'd barely gained three steps when the front bell rang—shrill and jarring. She turned back, heart stuttering with the foolish hope the Graybills had returned. Oh, to what depths she'd fallen.

Add to list: Hire the first available warm body with two working hands and no fear of imaginary rodents.

She set the linens on the front bench, then reached for the door—only to nearly lose her balance at the sight of the man on the front stoop.

Garbed from head to toe in black, the fellow regarded her with hard marble eyes, like a ghost with black holes for sockets. Sharp angles carved his jaw into a perpetual line of disapproval, and there was a cold aura about him, as if his slightest touch would freeze the flesh right off one's bones. A wispy hairline receded beneath an ebony top hat, and his lips were as thin as a ledger line, pressed tight as he studied her. He smelled inky and . . . metallic. Yes, that was it. He reeked of a fistful of coins that'd been squeezed too long.

She clung to the door, breath catching in her throat. A shiver of a whisper was the best she could manage. "Ben?"

"Belle?" He blinked, confusion rippling over his face like a pebble tossed into a pond. Perhaps it was the way he spoke her name—soft and unguarded—or the fleeting warmth that thawed the ice in his gaze. Just for a moment, the years melted away, and there stood the Ebenezer Scrooge she remembered. A handsome young man. The one who'd walked her home in the rain, laughing as he offered his coat. Dreaming of a future with her. Dancing at the Fezziwigs' Christmas ball.

But just as suddenly, the soft glow went out of his eyes, replaced by chilling calculation. He dipped a stiff bow. "Good day, Miss Beaumont. I did not know you were employed by Mrs. Trumble. I wonder if I might have a word with her?"

She clutched the door even tighter, the rough wood biting into her palm. He didn't know? Was he so preoccupied with his lifeless shillings that he took not a minute to inquire after the affairs of a woman whose property he was so eager to buy? Had he truly become that self-centered?

"Perhaps you ought to step inside, Mr. Scrooge." She opened the door wider, grieving for the inhuman shell this man had become.

He stepped past her with stiff precision, doffing his hat, and it was only then she noticed how gaunt he was—a coat hanging on bones, with thin wrists peeking out from his cuffs. One could not accuse him of gluttony—leastwise as far as food was concerned.

"This way, please." She led him down the corridor to her office, the creak of floorboards beneath their feet punctuating every step. It felt surreal, this meeting, as if a hole had been torn in time itself.

Once in her office, she circled her desk and gestured for him to take the chair in front of it.

He did so—warily—glancing about as if Mrs. Trumble might appear any moment. Yet he said nothing, apparently now as miserly with his words as he was with his coins.

Belle took her seat, folding her hands in front of her on the desk. "I regret to inform you that Mrs. Trumble died nearly a month ago. I am the new owner and director of Haven House."

"You?" His brows leapt. "But you were—" He stopped himself, yet even so, the unfinished thought hung in the air. She had been dowerless once, before her father had grown his business into a lucrative operation.

"Well . . . that is interesting," he said at length. "Good for you for rising up the ranks of society."

His grasping fingers tapped once on the arm of the chair before he shifted on the wooden seat. "I can only assume, then, that you have received my offer on the property."

"Yes, but what I do not understand is why you wish to own an orphanage. As I recall, you have no great love of children."

"Indeed." Dry laughter crumbled out like crushed leaves. "Would that the little urchins could start out in a proper pair of trousers instead of vile nappies." He sniffed disdainfully, his gaze flicking to the frost-glazed window behind her. "But since you ask, I have already acquired the Radcliffe House, your neighbouring parcel of land." He tipped his head toward that very window, as if he could see the outline of his new possession in the murk, then returned his gaze to her. "And with the acquisition of your property, there will be plenty of land for which to establish a large tenement, one that—if managed properly—will bring in quite the coin."

Ah. She might've known this was about lining his pockets.

"Profit, eh?" She leaned back in her chair, a wry smile twisting her lips. "I see you haven't changed."

"On the contrary." A predatory curve transformed the severe line of his mouth. His eyes narrowed, glittering like black glass. "I have learned a great deal over the past ten years, namely about what matters most, thanks to the tutelage of Mr. Marley. There is nothing more important than monetary security, Miss Beaumont. Contrary to popular thought, the world we live in does not run on sentiment."

"No," she said, heat flushing her cheeks. "It runs on the backs of children you would toss out to the street if it suited your books."

"A poor business practice, that. Street children earn next to nothing." He brushed an imaginary speck of lint from his sleeve. "Besides, I daresay with the income you'll make from the sale of this orphanage, those children of yours will be placed in bigger and better institutions, those that will provide more opportunity and education. One can only hope they will make the best of that advantage in their later years."

He pulled out a document from inside his coat pocket and—rising just a bit—placed it on her desk. "You can give them that chance, Miss Beaumont. A simple signature is all I need."

She stared at the purchase agreement, her heart thudding like a drum. This was a way out. A chance to stop worrying over repairs, over mice and fires, over Cricket's haunted eyes and Mrs. Bakewell's complaints. With funding like this, she could set the children up in a more affluent orphanage . . . but at the cost of wrenching the very heart from her chest. Despite all the chaos of the past month, she loved these children. Each one. Fiercely.

And for that reason alone, she picked up the pen and dipped it into the inkstand, hand trembling. "Very well, Mr. Scrooge."

But before she could touch nib to paper, Jack darted in. "Miss Beaumont!"

She glanced up, reading terror in the boy's eyes—from a twelve-year-old who feared nothing.

"Not now, boy!" Scrooge boomed. "Can you not see Miss Beaumont is occupied?"

She swallowed back her own fear, afraid to ask, but even more frightened not to. "What is it, Jack?"

"I always suspected you were a coddle-monger," Scrooge sneered. "You'd ruin these children were it not for me stepping in. Thank God you're making the right decision." He tapped his bony finger on the paper. "Just sign here and you can be about your business."

Jack flailed his arms. "Cricket is gone."

All the blood drained to her feet. "What do you mean 'gone'?"

Scrooge stabbed the paper all the harder, shoving it closer to her and upsetting a stack of portfolios in the process. "Sign here!"

Jack wagged his head, toe scuffing the floorboards. "I-I'm awful sorry. I know I been mean to him, but I ne'er meant for him to run away." He lifted his face, eyes shiny with tears. "I'm worried, miss. That little guppy ought not be out on the streets alone."

The pen clattered from her hand, leaving an ugly blotch on the document. "I beg your pardon, Mr. Scrooge. I have to see to this. Now."

She bolted from the room, skirts flying, leaving the man she once loved with nothing but an unsigned paper and the ghost of what might have been.

Sixteen

"Assure me that I yet may change these shadows you have shown me, by an altered life!"

—Charles Dickens, *A Christmas Carol*

She'd searched the whole house. They all had. Even little Birdie had crawled into spaces neither Belle nor any of the other children could fit into, calling softly, "Cricket? You hidin'?" as if her sweet little voice might coax him out like one of the kittens from a cupboard. But nothing. Not a sign of him. And with each passing hour, another piece of Belle's heart splintered. If she didn't find him soon, her chest would be nothing but an echo chamber, filled with guilt and the sound of one child's name spoken into silence.

Not even snow would remedy this tragedy.

Now here she was, on a dreary afternoon, bumping along in a hired hackney with a broken spring, a harsh December wind knifing in through the gaps in the door. It smelled of wet dogs in the cramped coach, making her eyes sting worse than the tears she kept battling. She snugged her coat tighter at the neck, trying to be grateful for small things like the warm wool and that her fingers still worked despite the cold. But gratitude was slippery this afternoon. She twisted her hands in the folds of her skirts, helpless and heartsick. Where was the boy?

Leaving the other children with Mrs. Bakewell to go find him felt like betrayal. And when she'd stopped off at the constabulary, it felt like being betrayed in return. The burly bluecoat had shrugged her off like an overanxious governess. "Boys run off all the time," he'd said. "It's a regular rite o' passage fer a lad o' five years. Give the nipper a week, and if he ain't back, then stop in again, and I'll sniff 'im out for ye."

A week? She couldn't help but snort a mist into the frigid air. Cricket didn't even know how to spell the word *week.*

Add to list: Resist the urge to hope the man steps on a loose cobblestone while carrying a full teacup.

The hack careened around a corner, lurching like a drunkard on skates, and she grabbed the cracked leather seat to keep from smashing against the wall. The Inns of Court couldn't be much farther. Hopefully. She had nowhere else to turn but to Rafe. And she would not—could not—think of the horror written on his face when she told him his nephew was gone.

If he was even back to the office yet.

She huffed on the window, melting a patch of frost, then cleared a small circle with the heel of her glove. But all she could see reflected in the glass was Cricket's lopsided smile, recently punctuated by the loss of his first tooth. Or the adorable way he tried to tie his little shoes. Hot tears burned her eyes. Were the boy's laces even now trailing like puppy-dog ears and tripping him as he wandered some frozen alley alone? Or was he hunched in a ball and shivering beneath a bridge somewhere?

A sob caught in her throat, a tormented sort of gurgle, and she turned her face to the wall, the wood biting cold against her temple. What kind of orphanage director failed the one child who most needed her to show abundant love?

A gust rattled the side window, the cold punching in like an accusation. Belle blinked hard. Unbidden, her father's voice floated up from the depths of memory, warm and steady . . .

"You have a way of carrying the world on those shoulders. You are neither Atlas nor the great Creator."

Hah! She couldn't even carry the pieces of one small boy's broken heart let alone keep the whole orphanage together.

"Make use of those He sends your way, and know I am ever at your beck and call."

Except he wasn't. Not this time. Her father was away on business until Christmas Day. And God? Well . . . He seemed out of reach at the moment too.

She grimaced, but still the words clung to her. Maybe Rafe was someone God had sent her way. Maybe she wasn't supposed to be Mrs. Trumble—meant to do this all alone. But if that was true, then why did the lesson have to be carved into her heart by the loss of a boy who only ever wanted to belong?

The carriage jolted to a stop, springs groaning a protest. The driver rapped twice on the roof. "Gray's Inn, miss."

After a quick dab at her eyes with the hem of her sleeve, she descended. The Inns of Court loomed before her with their stone archways framing narrow courtyards, the pungent sting of coal smoke thick on the air. Lawyers hurried by in their long coats and tall hats, none paying her any mind.

Squaring her shoulders, she stepped into the fray, heart thudding with dread—not just for Cricket but for Rafe's reaction.

She shoved open a carved wooden door and stepped into the warmth of an entry hall smelling of ink and old vellum. A faint trace of tobacco lingered like an afterthought. At the front desk sat a clerk with a round, ruddy face and a tidy white cravat. His spectacles slipped down the bridge of his nose as he looked up. "May I help you, miss?"

"Yes." She forced a small smile. "I wonder if you might direct me to the office of Mr. Rafe Munro?"

Slowly he shook his head, one beefy finger pushing the spectacles back where they belonged. "I am sorry, miss, but Mr. Munro is not currently in his office."

Her shoulders sagged. Of course he wasn't. For all she knew, a murder case could take days to resolve. She glanced at the polished floor, defeated, then murmured more to herself than to him. "I see. The Grindlethorn case must still be going on. Thank you."

Add to list: Don't cry—do not *cry—and pretend you're not unraveling like a hem caught on a nailhead.*

She turned to go—unsure where exactly—when a familiar voice caught her ear.

"I beg your pardon, but you are Miss Beaumont, are you not?"

"I am." She fixed her gaze on the approaching man with his ice-blue eyes and hump on his nose. Weariness dogged his steps, unlike the last time she'd seen him, when he'd marched up to Rafe and urged him away from caroling.

"You are Mr. Harvey," she said. "I recognize you from the other afternoon, when Mr. Munro joined the children and me for caroling."

A sheepish smile curved one side of his mouth. "Yes, I apologize for tearing him away like that." The small smile vanished. "Too bad it was for naught."

"Oh?" She angled her head, dread pooling in the pit of her belly. "Are things not going well in the courtroom at present?"

"More like past. A shameful defeat, that." He wagged his head sorrowfully, ending with a shrug. "The odds, as they say, were stacked against us. I suspect Munro could use a pretty shoulder like yours to lean against right now."

Her breath caught, her fingers fluttering to her throat. "Mr. Davis has been found guilty?"

"Unfortunately, yes."

Oh dear. Poor Mr. Davis. Poor Rafe. Was everything about this day to be nothing but sorrow upon sorrow? She pressed a hand to her middle, trying to stand tall in a world that seemed bent on spinning out of control.

"I . . . I thank you for the information, Mr. Harvey. Good day." She turned away, the floor tilting just slightly beneath her boots.

"Miss Beaumont?"

She glanced back.

"I suspect Munro has gone home. He might appreciate a listening ear—if he'll receive a visitor, that is. Worth a try."

She held his gaze for a breath, then nodded. "Thank you."

Outside, she hailed another hack, taking on the weight of Rafe's loss as well as her own. She couldn't imagine how the outcome in the courtroom had hit him, and now she was about to bring him even more unwelcome news. But what choice did she have? She couldn't traipse about London on her own, and without her father, Rafe was the most suitable escort.

And the only one who would understand the ache in her heart.

When the hack finally pulled up to his town house, her stomach had twisted into all sorts of knots, and that twisting only worsened when she stood in front of the Munro door and rang the bell. This time no mittened hand clung to hers. No cheerful voice asked questions. No Cricket.

The door opened to the same butler who'd admitted her to the open house. "May I help you, miss?"

"Yes, I—" She sucked in a fortifying breath of the cold air. "I wonder if Mr. Munro is at home."

"He is. Whom may I say is calling?"

"Miss Beaumont."

The man stepped aside, allowing her to pass into the front hall, which was every bit as prim and polished as it had been the night of the party. He swept out an arm, then pivoted on his heel. "Right this way, Miss Beaumont."

He led her to the sitting room, and the opulence of the place struck her all over again. The marble hearth. The velvet drapes. Oil paintings so grand they looked as if they belonged in a museum. It was quiet this time. No tittering voices of Mrs. Beesome and her sister or glasses clinking. Just the tick of a grand case clock in the corner. Without the laughter of party guests or the comfort of Cricket's small hand in hers, the room was too large and hollow.

She smoothed a gloved hand along her skirts, then turned at Rafe's deep voice.

"Belle?" He advanced, making a brave show of being put together, but all the same, she saw it. The droop of his broad shoulders. The tight lines at the side of his mouth. How defeat stole the usual spring in his step. "This is a surprise," he said simply.

"Oh, Rafe, I am so sorry about Mr. Davis. Mr. Harvey told me you lost the case."

His brow furrowed. "Where did you see Harvey?"

"At your office."

"You went to my office?" He cocked his head, the inquisitive barrister rising to the surface. "Why? Is everything all right?"

Before she could answer, his mother appeared in the doorway. Though she wore a simple blue day gown, she was every bit the elegant matron of the home. "I heard the front bell and—oh, Miss Beaumont."

Belle curtsied immediately. "Good afternoon, Mrs. Munro."

"Pardon me for interrupting." Rafe's mother dipped her head, a speculative yet wary glint in her eyes, then turned to leave.

Belle summoned what little courage she could find. "I-I think you should hear this too, Mrs. Munro."

Rafe's mother turned back, pausing just inside the threshold. Her hand rested on the doorframe, knuckles white. "Hear what?"

Oh, Lord, please grant favor!

Belle gripped the back of a nearby chair, fortifying herself for the storm that was surely about to blow in. "Cricket is missing. He disappeared after breakfast this morning."

"Missing!" Rafe thundered, stepping toward her so quickly a side table teetered behind him. "Are you sure? Did you—"

She shot up her hand. "The children and I, and even Mrs. Bakewell, searched every possible corner of Haven House. He is not there."

He paced two steps, then stopped. "What about the Graybills? Don't tell me they are missing again as well."

"I'm afraid they are gone for good. They left my employ the night I returned home from caroling."

"Blasted nincompoops," he muttered while rubbing the back

of his neck. He exhaled sharply, then stilled. "Did the boy leave a note?"

Pain thickened his voice, pain she'd do anything to remove. "He's five years old," she said gently. "Do you really think he'd take the time—or have the skill—to write something?"

"Oh dear." Mrs. Munro sank into the nearest chair. Her fingers fiddled with the clasp of her bracelet before falling limp in her lap, a faraway look glazing her eyes.

Rafe crossed to a sideboard and filled a glass of water. Without a word, he crouched before his mother and offered the drink.

Belle squeezed the hard wooden frame of the chair in front of her, powerless to know how to proceed. "I . . . I didn't know where else to turn. The law was no help, leastwise not for an orphan who's only been gone the better part of a day. I know he could turn up, but this just isn't like him. I'm worried."

"Of course you're worried." Rafe straightened, his tone now low and certain. "You have every right to be. I'll grab my hat and coat at once."

To Belle's astonishment, his mother stood as well, smoothing the folds of her skirt. "I will too."

Rafe gaped. "You are going to ramble about on the cold streets looking for a boy you do not wish to acknowledge?"

"Don't be absurd." She sniffed, already moving toward the door. "I shall go help this Mrs. Bakewell mind the children at Haven House while you two find the lad. He is, after all, my grandson."

Belle's breath caught in her throat. "That is very kind of you, madam. Thank you."

Mrs. Munro glanced over her shoulder, giving her a pointed look. "I realize you may think me heartless, Miss Beaumont, but I do know what it is to lose someone you love—and I wouldn't wish that on anyone."

Seventeen

"Nothing is past hope, if such a miracle has happened."
—Charles Dickens, *A Christmas Carol*

Darkness reigned, outside the coach and inside Rafe's heart. As the wheels rumbled along the quiet London streets on this late December eve, defeat bowed not only his shoulders but Belle's as well. Oh, how he longed to pull her against him and ease her worry. But he didn't dare. Not when his own heart was such a muddle. Every part of him ached with the need to find Cricket while fear raged that they might not. To hold Belle now—to seek comfort from her—would be selfish. Wouldn't it? In a sense, though, it might very well be his salvation.

He honestly wasn't certain.

Instead, he shifted on the seat, his breath a white mist in the cold air. He and Belle had searched into the darkest hours of night, visiting all the churches nearest Haven House, checking behind the bakeries, and poking about the laundress's courtyard. They'd looked into carts and every boy-sized crate behind the greengrocer's and even reluctantly walked the nearest Thames embankment, dreading to find a small body lying in the slushy water. Thank God Cricket had not been there!

Now, as the bells of St. Paul's chimed midnight, they were

heading back to Haven House on the off chance the lad had wandered home. And—if not—for another thorough upending of the building in case Belle and the children had missed a nook on the first search.

The wheels dipped into a rut, juddering the bones of them both.

"Blasted streets!" He righted Belle as she fumbled with the bonnet that'd slipped over her eyes. "I'd like to see the improvement commissioner drive a carriage down this road without needing a new set of teeth. I ought to sue the man for being so derelict in his duty!"

She laid a light touch on his sleeve, her eyes luminous in a shaft of light from a nearby streetlamp. "I'm sorry, Rafe."

He cocked his head. "These neglected roads are not your responsibility."

"No, I mean for today. For dragging you out like this after all you went through in court this morning. For . . . your loss."

The word *loss* went down like a mouthful of rancid meat. Davis, condemned by a system blind to truth, and Cricket, still missing. He'd failed them both. The weight of it all crushed the air from his chest, but Belle didn't need to hear about his burdens.

He attempted a smile. "You didn't drag me. I would have come anyway."

She gave his arm a little squeeze before folding her gloves in her lap. "Do you want to talk about it?"

"No." The word flew out, more abrasive than this woman deserved at such a time. She was only being kind, so he added softly, "But I will."

For a long moment, he rubbed the back of his neck, debating what to say—and what not. All the while she waited silently, nothing breaking the quiet but the rumble of the coach and the soothing cadence of her breath. It steadied him, that breath. Anchored him somehow in the dark.

"Davis didn't stand a chance," he began slowly, measuring each word, "not with that judge and prosecutor, but still

. . . I had hoped. That young man *is* innocent. Lord knows I tried my best to make the jury see that, but without some sort of proof to stand against Mrs. Hammer's testimony . . ." He shook his head, failure hot in his throat. "I just couldn't give them anything solid to refute her other than her questionable eyesight."

He stared at the floor of the carriage, jaw clenched against the storm inside him. "It wasn't enough."

"It's not your fault, Rafe." Her voice came gently.

His did not. "But it is!" He snapped his face toward hers. "Don't you understand that I failed that man? And I've failed before, God help me! Of course there are cases one cannot win, but when a man's life is on the line . . ." He tipped his head against the wall, gazing unseeing at the black ceiling. "I—" He swallowed hard. "I feel the weight of this one in my bones."

A light touch brushed against his hand. Gloved fingers, warm and sure, entwined with his.

"Then let me carry a little of it with you," she said simply.

He glanced down at her small hand pressed against his, and something fragile and fierce twisted in his chest. He hadn't expected such an intimate touch.

Then again, he hadn't expected her.

"Work like yours, Rafe," she continued, "is noble. Truly. But it's not the only important thing in life." A sigh feathered out of her. "I am coming to believe that maybe the Almighty didn't place us here solely to set the world aright. Rather, to love amidst the ruin. Even when it grieves us—or perhaps most when it does. For love may accomplish what justice, in all its forms, cannot."

He stared at her, moved. And completely disarmed. She spoke truth, all right.

Truth in love.

His heart swelled, ribs pressing up tight against his coat.

"You've a way of speaking honestly without making a man feel the fool," he murmured. "I . . . I've spent so long thinking duty was all. That if I worked harder, did better, I would attain a sort of perfection, I suppose." A bitter chuckle stuck in his throat. "But now . . ."

He fell silent, glancing at this brave, gentle woman who carried burdens of her own yet made room for his as well. What kind of man had he been, thinking duty and discipline were the whole of righteousness? When had he last allowed himself to want something purely for joy's sake? She was not merely a comfort. She was clarity. Lamplight on a foggy night. A star—*his* star, God willing. Oh, how weary he was of walking alone.

"And now?" she prodded.

"Now I find myself praying we find that boy safe so I can tell him he has a family. And . . ." He lifted her hand to his mouth and pressed his lips against the warm throb of the vein in her wrist. "I am wondering," he breathed the words against the sliver of exposed skin between glove and sleeve, "if a man like me might dare to hope for something more than friendship with a woman like you."

Her breath caught, the quiet hitch of it loud inside the dark coach.

"Far be it from me to dash a man's hopes." She smiled.

Silence bloomed between them, like a secret too precious to share with anyone but one's dearest love.

The coach jolted into another rut, breaking the moment—and nearly breaking them.

Belle pulled her hand from his, balancing with a grip on the seat cushion. "My! If we don't find Cricket soon, I may rattle apart entirely."

"You'll hold together." He grinned. "You are stronger than you think."

She wagged her head, a small smile curving her lips. "You are so like your sister. Jen used to say such things to Cricket. 'Hold fast, little Cricket, like Goody Two-Shoes. Brave as a lion, even when you feel like a mouse.'"

Instantly, Belle sat ramrod stiff, eyes widening.

Alarm jolted through him. "Belle? Are you all right?"

"That's it! *The History of Little Goody Two-Shoes* is Cricket's favorite story. He adores it, especially when the girl got her other shoe." She turned to him, bouncing on the seat. "He's gone to the cobbler on the next street over from the orphanage. I just know it!"

"Which one?" he asked, already leaning forward.

"Treadwell and Sons."

Without hesitation, he rapped sharply on the roof. "Driver, Treadwell and Sons. And step lively."

The horses surged forward, and a spare five minutes later, they clattered to a stop before a narrow shop front, its windows dark. Rafe leapt down first, then guided Belle to the pavement, his hand lingering against hers a moment longer than necessary.

Together they approached the door, and he pounded on it. Then pounded again. An eternity later, an elderly man in a frayed nightshirt and woolen socks blinked blearily through a crack in the door. "What's the ruckus?"

Rafe stepped forward. "We're looking for a boy about yea high." He held his hand around Cricket's height. "Goes by the name of Cricket. Have you seen him?"

The cobbler shook his head. "Can't say that I have, but if yer of a mind, ye may take a peek out back if ye like."

He widened the door, then led them through the dim shop, the scent of leather and beeswax thick on the air. Lantern in hand, he directed them past rows of half-finished shoes and tools, out to a yard.

Rafe and Belle called for the boy, poked into every shadow, looked in every dark crevice.

But no Cricket. Belle's spark of an idea had been for naught.

The cobbler escorted them back to the front door, where Rafe slipped a coin into the man's hand. Defeated, Rafe helped Belle up into the coach, then dropped into the seat beside her.

"Where to, sir?" the driver called.

Exactly. Where would the boy have gone? *Think. Think!* Another shoe shop, perhaps? One farther from Haven House? It was his favorite book, after all.

Wait a minute . . .

He turned to Belle. "What if it wasn't the shoes?"

Her brow wrinkled. "What do you mean?"

"What if it isn't the story but the book Cricket loves? Or rather the *books* Jenny read? I've frequently seen him with a book in hand despite the fact that he barely reads."

"Books?" Her eyes widened. "Books! Of course! Hatchards! I took the children there once on a special holiday away."

He practically punched the roof. "Hatchards!"

They jolted forward, wheels skidding slightly on the icy cobbles as they careened toward the bookshop on Piccadilly. They arrived to a building devoid of life. And this time there would be no kindly proprietor to see them around the back.

"Wait here," Rafe called as he jumped out.

"Not a chance." Belle practically leapt from the step.

With a chuckle, he grabbed her hand, keeping her upright, then swept her along as he circled around the building to the backside.

A handcart leaned against one side of the building. A barrel of refuse sat by a rear entrance. Farther on, a stack of broken crates teetered next to a coal chute.

Where a dirty-coated boy huddled next to it, shivering in the dark.

"Oh, Cricket!" Belle dropped to her knees, crushing the boy to her breast. Both their shoulders shook.

Rafe's chest squeezed at the sight. The boy looked so small—far too small to carry such sorrows. His breath came in ragged little puffs, his lashes clumped with soot and tears. He nestled close to Belle, as if trying to disappear. Rafe's throat burned. That was his sister's child. His family.

And only God knew what would have become of the child had they not found him.

At length, Belle set the boy from her, wiping his face with her thumbs. "Why did you run away, my sweet boy?"

He kicked his toe at a pebble. "Din't think anyone'd notice."

Rafe crouched next to Belle. "We noticed."

"Jack and Anne wouldn't." The boy's lower lip poked out.

"But Jack's the one who told me, darling." Reaching out, Belle brushed back a swath of the boy's hair. "We have all been so worried about you."

"You have?" He peeked at them.

And the wonder in his eyes nearly ruined Rafe.

Rafe nodded. "We've been all over London looking for you, young master."

"*All* over?" The boy blinked. "Caw! Din't think I mattered that much."

"You matter, my boy. More than you know. Cricket, I . . ." He gently laid a hand on the boy's shoulder, wanting—needing—to be connected more than just in words as he looked into that little face, all angles and smudges. "I should have told you sooner, lad, but I had to be sure. And now I am. I'm your uncle, young man. Miss Jenny—the one who read you books—was my sister. And she was your mother. Do you understand?"

He scrunched his nose—so like Jenny. "Miss Jenny were my mum?"

"Yes, and she loved you dearly. Fiercely. Which is why she came to Haven House every day. For you. For no one but you."

Cricket tipped his head, mouth twisting. "Then why din't she tell me?"

That was a huge question. One he could barely grasp himself. He looked to Belle, hating the helpless pleading that must surely be in his gaze.

She smiled gently and faced the boy. "Sometimes, Cricket, grown-ups think they're protecting someone when really they're just afraid. But Miss Jenny loved you, dear heart. So does Mr. Rafe, and so do I. So does everyone at Haven House."

"But Miss Jenny never once called me hers." The boy's words came out more bewildered than angry.

Rafe cleared his throat. It was either that or lose his dignity with a sob. "Because she didn't think she had the right. She'd made mistakes."

Cricket's chin dipped. "Guess I made one too. I din't mean to cause such trouble, Miss Beaumont, Mr. Rafe."

Rafe leaned close, crooking a finger and gently lifting the child's face so they were eye to eye. "That's Uncle Rafe to you, my boy."

"Really?" he whispered.

"Forever and ever."

"Even if I muck things up like Jack says?"

"Especially then." Rafe ruffled the boy's hair. "Family doesn't vanish when you make a mess of things."

"Come, love." Belle rose, holding out her hand to the boy. "Let's get you warm."

Rafe gave her a little shake of his head, then gathered the boy up into his arms like a lost lamb finally found. "Miss Beaumont is right. You've a snug bed waiting for you."

Cricket's arms looped around his neck, his head resting against his coat. He was all bones and shiver, this boy, but alive and breathing. Thank God! He breathed! Heart filled to bursting, Rafe held him close, as if he could press all the broken pieces of their lives back together, and led Belle around the dark bookstore to the waiting carriage.

Belle grasped the coach handle and stepped inside, then opened her arms to collect the boy. After directing the driver to Haven House, Rafe climbed in, Cricket tucked between them. Peace settled like God's embrace, and could he stop time, Rafe would live here in this safe cocoon, two souls he loved dearly at his side. And he marveled at just how much life could change in a mere month.

By the time they reached the orphanage, the lad leaned heavy against him, eyes closed, breaths even. Ever so gently, Rafe pried himself away, then hopped outside. Belle handed the sleeping boy over and exited herself.

Outside, frost silvered the fence railings and the rooftop. At the orphanage door, Belle turned to him. "I'll take him. Get your mother home, and we can speak of packing up Cricket's things in the morning if you like." She held out her arms.

He had barely transferred the boy over when the door opened. Rafe's mother didn't say a word as her gaze landed on the child. She didn't have to. There was no mistaking the love and longing welling in her eyes.

She stepped aside, one trembling hand rising to her mouth. "Thank God my grandson's been found," she whispered.

Belle crossed the threshold, whispering a weary thank-you to his mother, and carried the sleeping boy up the stairs. Rafe lingered in the hall, watching his mother as she closed the front door. She looked older tonight. Quieter. Still fragile, yet somehow stronger as well.

She smoothed her skirts, then glanced up the stairs, where the hem of Belle's coat disappeared. "He sleeps like Jenny did," she said softly. "Curled tight as a comma."

Rafe's breath stuck in his lungs. It was the first time she'd said his sister's name aloud since the funeral.

He flexed his fingers, weary of holding on to so much loss. Then again, had they not now found a priceless treasure as well? A grandson. A nephew. Maybe even the beginning of healing.

Funny, was it not, how the child who believed no one wanted him had become the one no one could bear to lose?

EIGHTEEN

> Scrooge never painted out Old Marley's name. There it stood, years afterwards, above the warehouse door: Scrooge and Marley. The firm was known as Scrooge and Marley.
>
> —Charles Dickens, *A Christmas Carol*

It was too much . . . certainly more than Belle could take. A sleepless night drowning in failure because Cricket had felt the need to run away. A morning barking orders like a madwoman, wrangling children into some semblance of proper human beings. And then Rafe had come to take away Cricket—and her heart had walked right out the door with the little boy in the too-big coat clinging to his hand. She'd been devastated. And so had the other children, particularly Rory and little Birdie, who'd known him all their lives. Even Jack had swallowed hard several times before running off to the playroom.

So here she now stood, cold and numb before a bleak shop front blackened by coal dust and the hard hearts inside. Overhead, a placard reading *Scrooge and Marley* swung by rusted chains in the biting December wind.

Oh, what a fool she'd been . . . and may be even now to make a deal with the man she'd cut loose all those years ago.

Belle gripped her reticule with both hands, trying to squeeze out the courage to waltz through that weathered slab of a door. Her breath ghosted in front of her, sharp and ragged. This shouldn't be so difficult. It was just a choice. Just a simple business transaction.

But it wasn't, not really.

It was the death of an illusion. A false belief that if she only worked hard and loved furiously she could make Haven House live up to its name. That she could provide the children with the best Christmas they'd ever experienced and make Mrs. Trumble proud she'd left the orphanage to a woman who could hold it all together.

But she hadn't. Her love hadn't been enough to keep Cricket from running away. Her hard work hadn't gotten the front room renovated, and quite frankly, if it hadn't been for Rafe, she'd not have organized the files either. She couldn't even keep the Graybills in residence. The Graybills, of all people! And now a boy she loved like her own was gone—off to a better life, yes—but gone all the same.

A wintry wind crawled in through her collar, chilling her to the marrow. The children deserved better than what she'd given them. They should live in a well-run home with plenty of staff to meet their needs. With Ben's generous offer, she could at least give them that.

Even if it meant going to the last place on earth she ever wanted to go.

Add to list: Locate backbone. Left it somewhere between this morning's cold bowl of porridge and little Birdie's pile of wooden blocks in the front hall.

Adjusting her gloves, Belle took a bracing breath, then tread the final steps across the snowless cobblestones to open the front door.

Inside the countinghouse, the air was thick with the scent of ink and old paper, and every bit as frigid. No wonder Jack Frost didn't paint the windowpanes here, for it was just as cold in the dimly lit receiving room as it was outside.

"May I help you, miss?" A clerk in a red woolen muffler

looked up from a ledger, where he sat at a tall desk off to the right, quill in hand.

"Yes. I should like to see—"

"Achoo!" The clerk turned barely in time before a huge sneeze escaped. Thankfully, or the pages in front of him would've been showered. And so would she.

"Pardon, miss. One moment." The man hopped off his stool, let loose another mighty sneeze, then dashed for a back door.

Odd, that. Did the fellow not carry a handkerchief?

She turned to the only other desk, but it was unoccupied as well.

Bother.

So she took a turn about the small room, keeping her blood flowing, and as she passed a cracked-open door on the opposite side, Ben's voice bellowed out.

"Don't tell me it was Smith! We both know better."

"All the same, sir," a deep voice answered, "Mr. Smith presented his token and collected the fourth payment. Thought you should know."

"Smith, my great giddy aunt!" Ben snorted. "If that man isn't Grindlethorn, then I'm a blasted bishop. Gait like a banker and a hook nose he can't disguise no matter how low he tugs his hat. And then there's that ridiculous token with the eagle—only Grindlethorn ever used such tactics, the old codswallop. My guess? He embezzled that widow's fund he was managing, then dumped it here under that absurd alias Thomas Smith, bland as a raw piece of toast. Marley said he was fleeing creditors, but I daresay it was the gallows. T. Smith can collect those monthly morsels without raising a single eyebrow. Clever devil. Dead men don't stand trial, after all."

Belle froze. *Grindlethorn?* The only time she'd ever heard such a distinctive name was in reference to Rafe's murder case. She dared a step closer to the door, listening hard.

Ben continued, his voice lower but still audible. "The man has one more visit scheduled for the night before Christmas, and he's done. I'm of a mind to exploit that somehow, perhaps squeeze him for my silence. But . . . is that cockroach really worth my time? And if he's recognized, we cannot have him leading the law to our door. Mr. Marley would have my head on a platter like a festooned boar for his Christmas dinner. And he'd enjoy every bite."

An oily chuckle followed, thick with amusement.

The deep voice responded, "Now that you are apprised of the situation, is there anything else I can do for you, sir?"

"Yes. I should like—"

Belle turned away, pulse pounding, and dashed the few steps to the vacated desk in front of Ben's office. As she'd hoped, a ledger sat open. With a quick glance around to be sure the clerk with a cold hadn't returned, she snatched it up and scanned column after column, her gloved fingertip darting down the page until . . .

There.

Mr. T. Smith

Token: eagle pendant

Depositor Note (Sept. 1): Transfer of remainder from W.H. Benevolence Trust

Withdrawals: Sept. 21, Oct. 25, Nov. 27, Dec. 21

Final Withdrawal Due: Dec. 24

She stared at the page, barely breathing. Grindlethorn hadn't just stolen money—he was about to disappear with the last of it.

And poor Ward Davis was about to pay for it with a life of exile.

Rafe needed to know.

Now.

Rafe stood in his office, the shutters half-drawn against the dismal afternoon. A wintry wind rattled the glass panes. Such a lonely sound. As empty as his soul at the moment. Was he making the right decision?

His red bag, now half-empty, lay open on the desk beside a stack of briefs he'd no longer be arguing. He slipped another book into the satchel—the old Blackstone he just couldn't part with—then paused, fingers lingering on the leather.

Ward Davis's face had haunted his dreams since the verdict. That horrified widening of the young man's eyes. His mouth gaping in a silent scream. Davis had not received justice, only convenience wrapped in ceremony. Though he'd tried, Rafe hadn't been able to right such a horrible wrong . . . but by all that was holy, he'd do all he could to right the world for the little boy he'd brought home this morn. He couldn't change Cricket's past, that much was certain, but he could control the world the boy lived in now.

And that didn't include Rafe standing in courtrooms for hours on end, defending a system that let monsters roam free while condemning innocents. He had no illusions left about the law's power to save everyone. But neither would he pretend that clinging to his post, grinding himself into the dust, was the only path God could use. Others could take up the fight in the courts—men with fresh strength and unjaded eyes. His work, for now, would be in the shadows, helping where the law could not—or would not—go. A change of battlefields, so to speak. He just had no idea what or where his place would be.

Though a certain home for London's forgotten children tugged persistently at the back of his mind.

Footsteps approached, and soon Harvey leaned against the doorframe, arms crossed, brows drawn. "You're serious, then?" He nodded at the now-empty bookshelves. "You're going to throw away your whole blasted career because one case didn't go your way?"

Rafe frowned. "It's more than that, and you know it."

"Dash it all, Munro! You cannot win them all."

"I cannot win any if the court is going to feed innocent men to rabid wolves while we watch in wigs and robes."

"Such dramatics." Harvey shook his head. "It's tragic, I agree. We live in an imperfect world, but such is the cost of the game. You know that."

"I'm done playing." He shut the satchel, buckling it closed with a finality that rubbed him raw.

"So," Harvey remarked, "what will you do instead? Take up preaching? Open a bakery, perhaps? Will that solve your problems? You think you're going to make the world fair by quitting and doing something else?"

"No." Rafe shoved in his chair. "But I'll start by not being complicit in its cruelty. I've got a child to look after now. Cricket needs someone steady in his life. Someone honest. I can show him how to walk away when a thing becomes too rotten to fix." He paused, then added quietly, "The law still needs good men—honest men—but I am not the one to shoulder it just now."

"And you're saying I am?" Harvey let out a dry laugh. "Have you ever considered that even rot serves its purpose? A dung heap is the beginning of a lush garden, after all."

Rafe cocked his head, a wry grin twitching his lips. "Waxing philosophical, are you? Didn't know you had it in you, man."

Hefting a huge sigh, Harvey stepped away from the door and planted his hands on Rafe's desk, leaning toward him. "The truth is, Rafe, this firm needs you. *I* need you. You're the best up-and-coming barrister there is. I'll speak to the powers that be and see about getting you less cases to work on. Take off a few weeks, clear the cobwebs from your head, and then—"

"Rafe! Thank heaven you're here!" Belle burst into his office, cheeks flushed, eyes bright, the scent of wintry air and ginger wafting about her as she tried to catch her breath.

"Belle? What has happened?" Alarmed, he advanced, taking hold of her arm to guide her to a seat.

She merely pulled away, head wagging. "There's no time for sitting right now. There's too much to say. We must plan! We must pull together a contingency of officers and—"

"Calm down, Miss Beaumont," Harvey cut in, eyebrows

raised. "Your rambling is making Munro here ready to charge out and fight the world on your behalf."

He was. God help him, he was.

Belle straightened, fire flashing in her eyes. "And I am thankful he is the sort of man who thinks the world is worth fighting for. But enough banter." She turned to Rafe, and when her gaze locked on his, something unspoken passed between them—something that made his heart leap. "I've recently left Scrooge and Marley's countinghouse, where I—"

Rafe shot up a hand, his earlier alarm now magnified. "Don't tell me you've sold Haven House! I know it's been rough on you, but I can help you manage now."

She blinked, then shook her head. "No, I didn't. I mean, I was going to. I walked in there with every intention. But then I overheard a clerk speaking with Mr. Scrooge in his office. He mentioned a man collecting his final payment—with an eagle token."

Rafe furrowed his brow. "I assume you have some point with all this."

Harvey chuckled. "Give her time, man. Women like their little intrigues."

That earned him a glower from Belle, yet she continued, "Mr. Scrooge believes the man cashing in those tokens is Mr. Grindlethorn. He said as much. The man is alive, Rafe! Mr. Scrooge thinks he faked his own demise to avoid being caught at embezzlement."

Rafe stared, hardly comprehending her words. Belle's voice still echoed in the room, but he could only hear the pounding of his heart. If that was true . . .

"You're certain?" he asked.

She nodded vigorously. "I saw the ledger for myself. He's scheduled to come in one last time on Christmas Eve. We could catch him! We could prove beyond the shadow of a doubt that Mr. Davis is innocent. This could undo everything!"

Harvey blew a low whistle. "Well, I'll be hanged."

For the first time in twenty-four hours, Rafe breathed. Really breathed, the heavy chains that'd clamped his chest falling away. Joy, hope, light—all surged through his veins.

He grabbed Belle by the arms and swung her around, letting out a whoop. She laughed, breathless and radiant, and for the briefest moment, he was no longer in a dingy office but some sunlit dream. He wanted to kiss her—desperately—but Harvey was watching. And Belle deserved better than impulse.

He set her from him, rubbing his hands together. "That gives me three days to alert the constables and figure out the most strategic spot to lie in wait."

"You mean that gives *us* three days."

"No," he said gently. "It's too dangerous. I need you safe. This isn't a charity auction or a dinner party. If Grindlethorn faked his death, who's to say he won't kill to keep that secret?"

She lifted her chin, jaw set. "I'm involved now, whether you like it or not. With or without your blessing, I will see justice carried out."

Stubborn woman! Brilliant, vexing, irresistible woman. He funneled his fingers through his hair, thoroughly frustrated—and not just a little in love with her for it.

Harvey chuckled. "Well, I certainly wouldn't be the one to tell her no."

Rafe dragged his hand down his face, muttering a prayer under his breath. May God help them—because one way or another, Grindlethorn was going to answer for what he'd done.

Or Rafe would die in the trying.

Nineteen

Once upon a time—of all the good days in the year, on Christmas Eve—old Scrooge sat busy in his counting-house.

—Charles Dickens, *A Christmas Carol*

Three days later, Belle inhaled the frosty evening air, invigorated not just by the chill but from the nearness of Rafe Munro—solid and silent at her side, his coat brushing hers in the dark. They crouched in the narrow alley just opposite Scrooge and Marley's, half-shielded by a stack of delivery crates and the deep shadows of a boarded-up milliner's shop. If Father knew she was here, huddled next to a man without a chaperone—unless one counted the two nearby constables also in hiding—he'd suffer an apoplexy. Or start planning a wedding, the way he'd been scheming about the two of them. But Father wouldn't be home until close to midnight, which was several hours off.

And hopefully, this whole sordid affair would be over by then.

Her gaze drifted to the countinghouse, where a single candle flickered in Ben's office. The rest of the building was as black as a crypt. It was a lonely sight, one that ached in her heart. She didn't love him—not the way she loved Rafe—but she pitied him. To spend Christmas Eve hunched over ledgers while others gathered around fires, singing hymns or telling stories, was a sorrow she wouldn't wish on anyone. He should be at church. Or home. Anywhere but here, clutching wealth that could never keep him warm. If he didn't change his ways, he would die a lonely old man with no one to mourn him. She shivered at the thought.

Add to list: Things I never want to become—rich and lonely.

"You're cold." Rafe's low voice rumbled in her ear. Without waiting for permission, he pulled her closer to his side. "You should be at home with the children."

Belle didn't resist. She should be at Haven House, playing blind man's bluff or reading a festive tale—but somehow, being here with the man she'd so quickly grown to love felt more right than anything else. Though he'd not said as much, she suspected that deep down he appreciated her support in bringing justice to an innocent man.

"I admit," she said softly, "this isn't quite the Christmas Eve I envisioned for the children, but thanks to your mother hiring Mrs. Kincaid, I suspect they're blissfully knee-deep in gingerbread and honeyed cider."

Rafe chuckled. "So the new matron is working out, then?"

"She's only been there two days, but so far she hasn't run off screaming."

He tilted his head. "Or brought in any extra goats or turnips?"

"Not even any medicinal ferrets." She smirked.

His brow wrinkled. "Medicinal ferrets?"

"Don't ask."

He huffed a quiet laugh, the sound low and warm in the winter stillness.

She scanned the street—still empty—then murmured, "Maybe Grindlethorn isn't coming. Do you think he knows we're lying in wait?"

"He'll come." Rafe's voice turned hard. "A rat always returns to the pantry."

A carriage clattered by in the distance. An alley cat yowled. But no shadow slinked toward the countinghouse.

She turned to Rafe. "How is Cricket settling in?"

His teeth flashed white in a grin. "In the boy's own words, 'No one's yelled at me, no one's pinched my socks, and I didn't have to dodge a swipe from Jack even once.' So I think it fair to say, he's loving it. And naturally, he's won over not only my mother but the entire staff."

Her chest squeezed in a familiar ache of bittersweet joy. She missed the lad—terribly—and yet there was no better place on earth for him than the Munros' home. She peered up at Rafe. "And the adoption paperwork? How long before you're legally his guardian?"

"If I work through tomorrow, it should be finalized by early next week."

"Tomorrow?" Her jaw dropped. "But, Rafe, it's Christmas!"

He gave her a mock-serious look, eyes glinting. "It's either paperwork at my desk or chaos and caroling at Haven House with your lot."

"You're jesting." She smacked him playfully on the arm. "Beast."

He chuckled. "Is that what you think of me?"

"Of course not." She leaned closer, breathing in his manly scent of bay rum aftershave. "Beasts have better manners."

"Teasing, are we?" He arched a brow.

She gave a sly smile. "Only a little. Besides, someone has to keep your ego in check."

He slapped an affronted hand to his chest. "You think I have an ego?"

"I think you have a great many things, Rafe Munro. Stubbornness. Swagger. A dangerous tendency to make a lady forget her better judgment."

His gaze dropped to her lips, and a flicker of longing crossed his face. "And what does your judgment say now, hmm?" His voice became husky as he closed what little distance remained between them.

She swallowed, heart suddenly racing. He was but a breath away. One. Single. Breath.

But now was definitely not the time.

She glanced away.

Only to see movement. A figure keeping close to the storefronts, hat pulled low, collar turned high.

"Look," she whispered, inclining her head ever so slightly toward the approaching man in an ankle-length greatcoat. "Is that—"

But Rafe was already gone.

This was it. Justice within reach—literally. Rafe lunged, throwing his full weight against Grindlethorn, and rode him to the ground. Hard.

A burst of colourful curses exploded on the night air as the scoundrel twisted beneath him. "Get off me!"

"Not a chance," Rafe growled, pinning the man's arms.

Grindlethorn bucked like a lunatic. One arm broke free, and a gloved fist connected with Rafe's nose. Hot blood streamed over his lips.

The blighter!

Boots pounded toward them as they rolled over the cobblestones.

"Oi!" one of the constables shouted. "That's enough o' that!"

But Grindlethorn wouldn't quit. He roared and heaved sideways, driving a boot straight into Rafe's ribs.

"Rafe!" Belle cried, her voice a shiver in the shadows.

Gasping for air, Rafe staggered to his feet, grabbing hold of Grindlethorn's collar before the cully could get away. "Give it up, man. You're not going anywhere but to the gallows."

The villain thrashed again, bellowing oaths. "You can't prove a thing!"

Before the rogue could swing another fist, the constables flanked him. One swiped a club to the back of his knees, dropping Grindlethorn to the ground. "Save it for the magistrate, ye scurf," the bluecoat spit out.

"You're making a mistake!" Grindlethorn squawked. "I'll sue every last one of you for assault."

The other constable guffawed and flipped him like a sack of oats, iron clinking as he secured the shackles on his wrists. "Go ahead. Ye'll get but two shillings out of me—and that's if you catch me sober."

His partner stepped in, hauling Grindlethorn roughly to his feet, the man shouting epithets coarse enough to make a sailor wince.

Just then, a door creaked open across the lane. The golden glow of a lone candle spilled into the night, stretching long shadows over the stoop. A lean figure emerged from Scrooge and Marley's, his features thrown into sharp relief by the flickering light. "What's all this infernal humbug? A body can hardly work! Off with you! Or I'll call down the law."

"We are the law," one constable muttered, giving Grindlethorn a hearty shove that sent him moving forward.

"This is not to be borne!" Scrooge barked, shaking a fist at the heavens. "I demand peace and quiet, as has been rightfully purchased by my taxes."

Rafe swiped the blood from his nose with the back of his sleeve, shooting Scrooge a withering look. "If you'd prefer that thieves roam free, you are welcome to file a complaint with my law office."

"I prefer to be left alone!" He turned on his heel so swiftly, the flame went out. He stomped blindly into the countinghouse with a great slam of the door.

Belle rushed to Rafe's side, worry creasing her brow. "Are you all right?"

He wiped the last smear of blood from his nose and gave a wry smile. "I am now. That monster's headed where he belongs." He tipped his head toward the constable strong-arming Grindlethorn into the back of a dark wagon.

"We'll see this scourge safely locked away, Mr. Munro." The other constable tipped his hat before climbing to the driver's seat. "And a merry Christmas to you both."

"Merry Christmas," Belle and Rafe echoed together.

Their eyes met—and held as the grind of the prison cart's wheels faded away.

Then, as if heaven itself had been holding its breath all this time, a snowflake drifted lightly down. Right there, in front of a miserly countinghouse on a bleak street absent of any sort of holiday cheer. It was followed by another. And another. Until soon, a splurge of flat flakes floated about like little fairies.

Belle lifted her face to the sky, wonder widening her big brown eyes. Her hands raised as though receiving a benediction meant for her alone. "Oh," she breathed, her delight as pure as an angel song. Her lashes fluttered as the flakes landed on her cheeks, her hair, her lips. Radiance beamed off her, achingly beautiful. A woman men would die for.

Rafe's chest tightened. Without even being aware, she undid him. The softness of her. The resilience.

And he could take it no longer.

He gathered her close, one hand cupping her cheek, the other settled at her waist—and kissed her. Tenderly. Fiercely. Her breath hitched. His heart slammed. She leaned into him like she'd been waiting for this as long as he had. And in that moment, there on a dark London street, the world tilted more toward right than ruin. He would never be the same. He was a new creation now. A new man. Remade in a way he'd never imagined by the simple love of the woman in his arms.

Church bells broke over the city, a carillon heralding the arrival of Christmas, ushering in the holy day of miracles.

Twenty

"God bless us every one!"
—Charles Dickens, *A Christmas Carol*

Snow! Glorious snow. Pillowed atop the fence rail. Covering the sins of soot and softening all the edges of a city grown harsh with use. The fresh white blanket muffled the noise, stilled the rush, and turned every rooftop into a storybook. It was here. Finally! And on Christmas Day, no less. Belle grinned so wide her cheeks ached as she stared out the playroom window on Christmas morn.

Behind her, the children spun their new tops and cradled cloth dolls—gifts her father had brought when he'd arrived for breakfast. Mrs. Bakewell had outdone herself with a feast of warm oatcakes, spiced apple compote, and thick slices of treacle bread slathered in butter. She'd even warmed the milk with chocolate, crowning each mug with a dollop of whipped cream.

And yet none of it—not the snow, the feast, or even the merriment of the children's laughter—held a candle to the memory of Rafe's sweet kiss last evening. Heaven help her, she'd hardly slept for reliving it! How right it had been to be held in his arms. To thrill at the look of love sparking in his eyes. The fierce tenderness of it all. Her heart had yet to settle. She pressed her fingertips to her lips, holding the memory in place.

"You're doing it again." Her father's voice curled over her shoulder.

She spun, arching a brow. "You, of all people, should know I cannot help but smile at the snow."

He shook his head. "That's not what I'm talking about. I meant that rosy hue rising on your cheeks every time you chance a touch to your mouth. I've been gone for several days. . . . Is there something I should know about?"

That she was falling madly in love with Rafe Munro?

That he kissed like a man who'd staked his claim and would make it last a lifetime?

That she'd been half-afloat ever since?

No. She couldn't very well say any of that to her father. Clearing her throat, she squared her shoulders. "Sometimes you must allow a woman her secrets, Father."

"Then to be fair, you must allow me mine." He waggled his eyebrows.

"*You* have secrets? How novel!"

"Perhaps I shall tell you of them one day. But for now"—his voice softened—"there is one matter of which I should like you to clear up. Namely, what have you decided about Mr. Scrooge's offer to purchase the orphanage?"

A top spun wildly across the floor, tangling in her hem. She bent to retrieve the runaway and handed it back to a ruddy-cheeked Pippin, who'd skittered over to her as fast as the toy.

"Thank you, Miss Beaumont."

"You're welcome." She patted the child on the head, then straightened to face her father. "I have decided to decline Ben's offer once and for all."

He studied her a moment, face inscrutable. "And your reason?" he said simply, giving not a hint of his feelings on the matter.

She lifted her chin. "Because I've come to realize this place—with all its chaos and cacophony—isn't a burden. It's a calling."

Her gaze drifted to the children tumbling about like a litter of pups. "So I am officially letting go of trying to make Haven House perfect and am choosing instead to make it a place of love."

A slow grin spread on his face. "I think, my dear, there could be no better reason."

Just then a whoop went up. Both she and her father turned to see the Munros—Rafe, his mother, and Cricket—each carrying paper-wrapped parcels and some bags. A few small packages trailed on the floor behind Cricket.

Belle stepped away from the window. "What's all this?"

"Presents!" shouted Cricket, bouncing on his toes. He ran to Jack, a gap-toothed smile lighting his face as he handed over a long package. "I've got a special one just for you."

Mrs. Munro approached her, kissing the side of her cheek in greeting. Up close, Belle caught sight of a brooch fastened at the lady's collar—a delicate gold cross with a single pearl at the center. The same one that'd been in Cricket's file—the one Rafe said had belonged to his sister. Belle's breath caught. He must've had it fashioned into a pin for his mother.

And the thoughtfulness of that weakened her knees. How many men would even think of such a gesture?

"Merry Christmas, my dear." Mrs. Munro took her hands and gave her fingers a little squeeze. "You have no idea how good it feels to say that *and* mean it."

Belle squeezed her back. "I think I do."

"Perhaps not to the same depth. Since my husband's and daughter's deaths, I stopped living, but now that my grandson has been restored to me—" Her voice cracked, and she dabbed her eyes with a lacy handkerchief. "Well, suffice it to say, I believe this is the best Christmas ever. Rafe may have given me a lovely brooch . . ." She fingered the ornate pin, love glowing on her face as her gaze drifted to Cricket. "But that child is the piece of Jenny that truly mends my heart."

"Oh boy! A wooden sword!" Jack's bellow interrupted the poignant moment. He brandished his new weapon in the air, then just as suddenly, dropped it to his side, face twisting. "But . . . why would you give me such a good gift, Cricket? I—I've not been the kindest mate to you, I admit."

Cricket's smile grew. "That's okay. My uncle gave me one too. Now we can fight on the same side. That's better, ain't it?"

Jack's shoulders slumped. "I . . . I've never had a partner before."

"Then we better start practicing." Cricket raced over to Rafe, who silently produced a duplicate sword from a sack—but the twinkle in his eye said loud and clear that he remembered what it was to be five and fearless.

He wagged a finger at both Cricket and Jack. "Mind you take care with those swords. Don't damage any goods or other children, hmm?"

"Yes, Mr. Munro." Jack nodded vigorously, then turned to Cricket with a shy grin. "Ready, partner?"

The two whacked their wooden blades together with a satisfying crack, then took off across the room, dodging furniture like knights on a quest.

Belle's heart swelled at the sight. How good it was to hear laughter instead of sniping!

The other children clamored over to her father and Mrs. Munro, hands full of new picture books. "Read us a story?" they said in unison.

The two older adults couldn't look more pleased as they settled on the sofa amidst a tangle of small elbows and knees.

"That's our cue to exit stage right," Rafe whispered in her ear while tucking her hand in the crook of his arm.

He led her just past the threshold and stopped in the front corridor, within ear range of the playroom yet wholly more private. Her heart raced. Was he going to kiss her again?

But instead, he produced a small scroll from his pocket and handed it over.

Her brows knit as she untied the red ribbon securing the roll. But of course. This must be Cricket's adoption papers. He'd likely gotten them early and wished to share the good news.

She paused before opening the pages and glanced up at Rafe. "How did you manage all this? I doubt you slept a wink. I assume Mr. Grindlethorn is behind bars and Mr. Davis is free?"

He shrugged. "Heroes don't need sleep."

She rapped him on the arm with the scroll.

He laughed. "All right. Fine. I'm half-asleep on my feet. But, yes, with Grindlethorn's confession, Davis is cleared. Turns out the old tight fist faked his own death, going so far as to purchase a corpse to burn in his place, all to avoid getting caught for siphoning funds from a widow's release trust he'd been managing. He slipped the money into a discreet account at Scrooge and Marley's under the name T. Smith and took monthly payouts—just enough to keep things quiet."

She cocked her head. "And the eagle token?"

"His proof of identity. No paper trail, no name. Just that token and the silence of Scrooge and Marley. If you hadn't overheard that snippet of conversation and noticed that ledger entry . . ." He trailed off, pensive for a moment, then he said quietly, "I've been thinking that for far too long I've carried the whole of justice on my shoulders, as if it depended upon me alone. You—and God—have shown me otherwise. I can't save every soul the courts forget, but perhaps that's not my job. All I can do is take the cases that matter most and fight them the best I am able, then trust the rest to the One who's sovereign even over law. And so I shall keep my barrister's gown, though not wear it quite as often, for when I am not in court, I hope to be here with you." He glanced toward the playroom and back to her. "And with them."

Her breath caught.

"Now," he said, a corner of his mouth tipping upward, "are you going to open that scroll, or shall I?"

Smiling through a sudden prickle of tears, she smoothed out the paper and held it up.

Aha. So it was a legal document!

To Whom It May Concern:

Be it known on this date, the twenty-fifth of December, in the year of our Lord 1819, that I, Rafe Munro, barrister of law and of sound mind (though hopelessly ensnared of heart), do hereby submit the following declarations:

1. *That I have formally commenced the adoption proceedings for one Jonathan Cricket Munro (so named and so cherished), and by this action pledge myself as both guardian and uncle in all ways that matter and shall endure.*
2. *That I intend, with earnest purpose and heartfelt affection, to seek the courtship of Miss Isabelle Beaumont with the honourable aim of securing her hand in marriage, should she regard my suit with favor.*
3. *That I pledge my full willingness to join Miss Beaumont in partnership and shared purpose at Haven House, that together we might continue its good work in unity of heart to the benefit of the children.*

Let this document stand as proof not of legality alone but of devotion, intent, and a future freely chosen and hoped for.

Most earnestly and
entirely yours,

Rafe Munro

Her breath caught in her throat as she reread every single word, for to do anything other than commit them to memory would be a great loss.

Then she read it again.

And again.

"You're making me wait a very long time, Miss Beaumont," Rafe murmured low, voice husky. "Unless I was mistaken in that kiss we shared last night?"

She tipped her face to his, her pulse a maddening beat in her ears. "If that was a mistake, then by all means, make another."

A roguish grin curved his lips. "I assume that can only mean you agree to my suit?"

Stepping closer, she smoothed her fingers along his lapels, enjoying far too much his sudden intake of air at her touch. "It means, barrister, that I've already imagined your name as my own far too many times."

"Well, then, merry Christmas." His lips came down gently on hers.

The front door burst open. A gust of wind ushered in a blast of cold, a blanketing of snow—

And Joe and Betty Graybill.

Belle pulled away, blinking. Along with her satchel, Betty carried a chicken in a bonnet tucked into the crook of her arm. Joe hefted a lumpy sack over one shoulder, a hurdy-gurdy hung by a strap on the other.

"We're back!" Joe hooted.

"Aye, here we are!" Betty chimed in. "Turns out my sister's house didn't suit us a bit. She's got a cat with a glass eye that follows a body around the room, and Joe's still shedding like a molting goose from her lye soap."

"That and she didn't appreciate our creativity, not like you do, Miss Beaumont." Joe tipped his hat, then slung his sack onto the floorboards. "And we're here just in time for Christmas cheer. We've brought gifts for one and all."

At the word *gifts*, the children spilled out of the playroom and crowded about them.

Joe opened the canvas to reveal an assortment of dented tin spoons, some broken gingerbread men, a few heads of cabbage, one very wrinkled scrap of muslin, and what looked suspiciously like a taxidermied squirrel wearing spectacles.

Which was, of course, the first item snatched up.

Shrieks and laughter filled the hall like warm lamplight, bright and golden, wrapping around Belle's heart. She glanced up at Rafe, whose hand had found hers, his fingers steady and sure as he gave hers a squeeze.

This house—with its still-burned-out front room, a smattering of endless-energy children, and caretakers Belle could only smile at—rang with joy. The future would not be perfect, she knew that, but it would be full. Full of stories. Full of tears and laughter.

And most importantly, full of love.

She leaned into Rafe's side and whispered, "Merry Christmas."

He kissed the top of her head. "And may God bless us with many more to come."

Add to list: Keep this Christmas—and every one thereafter—tucked away in my heart.

Historical Notes

Belle from *A Christmas Carol*

Everyone thinks they know who Belle is, but how much of that is based on the original text? Surprisingly, Hollywood paints our picture of the woman in embellished ways that Dickens never mentioned. Here is exactly what we know about her from the original manuscript of *A Christmas Carol*:

- Belle appears only in stave two.
- She was Scrooge's fiancée but broke it off when he became obsessed with wealth.
- Dickens calls her "a fair young girl in a mourning-dress" and later gives her a name.
- She's described as dowerless (not poor) but with no backstory or family name.

Society for Bettering the Condition and Increasing the Comforts of the Poor

This organization was founded in 1796 by Sir Thomas Bernard and other reform-minded philanthropists. It aimed to promote practical solutions to poverty through improving housing, education, childcare, and employment opportunities. Rather than relying solely on charity, the society encouraged self-help and community-based initiatives.

Negus

Negus—a mixture of wine, hot water, sugar, lemon, and nutmeg—was quite a popular holiday beverage in England. It was served at gatherings, assemblies, and charitable receptions. The drink is said to be named after Colonel Francis Negus, who introduced the refreshment in the early eighteenth century. Its gentle sweetness and festive spice make it a particular favorite at Christmas.

Saint Nicholas Day

Celebrated on December sixth, this day honors the fourth-century bishop known for his generosity and kindness, particularly toward children and the poor. In many European countries, children place shoes or stockings out the night before in hopes of finding small gifts, sweets, or coins left by Saint Nicholas. This tradition helped shape the modern figure of Santa Claus.

Posset

A posset is a warm, creamy drink made from milk or cream curdled with wine or ale and laced with sugar and spice. Once a medieval remedy for colds and sleeplessness, by the early 1800s it had become a treat, often served at Christmas or after supper, when spirits ran high and the night ran long.

Christmas Markets

In the weeks leading up to Christmas, outdoor markets sprang up in various parts of London, offering a wide array of festive goods and treats. Market stalls sold seasonal foods, such as roasted chestnuts, mulled wine, gingerbread, and other sweets, as well as handcrafted gifts, decorations, and greenery. This tradition lives on even today.

Red Bag

The red bag Rafe carries isn't just a fashion statement. A barrister's red bag is a traditional gift given by a King's or Queen's Counsel (depending upon who is on the throne at the time) to a junior barrister in recognition of exceptional work, often after assisting on a significant case. Made of crimson leather or fabric, the bag is both a symbol of esteem and a practical item used to carry legal papers in court.

Discussion Questions

1. The story begins with waiting before anything changes. When has waiting shaped your life more than the moments of action?
2. Belle holds herself to very high standards and feels a deep responsibility for Haven House. Naturally, this adds a lot of internal stress to an already stressful situation. Has there been a time in your life when you held unreasonable expectations of yourself? How did you deal with it—or wish you'd dealt with it?
3. Like Rafe, have you ever stayed in a role or responsibility longer than was healthy because walking away felt like failure?
4. Grief makes Mrs. Munro withdrawn where she was once more outgoing. Now she rarely leaves the house. Has grief ever shaped a choice you made the way it does Mrs. Munro's?
5. Cricket feels like no one listens to him or sees him. Has there ever been a time in your life when you felt invisible?
6. Have you ever had a moment—like Rafe losing the case—when something falling apart clarified what actually mattered?

7. Haven House is never fully fixed, only loved. What in your life has remained messy but meaningful?
8. Faith is present but quiet throughout the novel. Where do you see trust in God expressed through action rather than words?
9. In Dickens's works, children often see truth more clearly than adults. What does Cricket understand that the adults around him miss?
10. Christmas imagery appears long before Christmas Day. What moments felt most Christmas-like to you, and why?

Acknowledgments

Three cheers to Rochelle Gloege, Kate Deppe, and the fine folk at Bethany House Publishers. You've taken this humble story, brushed off its soot, and sent it out as shiny as a new shilling in Christmas pudding.

A raised glass of negus to my agent, Wendy Lawton, of Books & Such Literary Management—a true friend of words and Dickens.

To my merry band of ink-slinging compatriots—Angela Bell, Kendall Hoxsey, Tara Johnson, Julie Klassen, Shannon McNear, Ane Mulligan, Chawna Schroeder, MaryLu Tyndall, Erica Vetsch—you take my tangled words, smooth them out, and somehow make me look like I know what I'm doing.

A tip of the ol' top hat to my dear readers. There are too many to name, but in each book I love to mention a few. So here's to you Joanne Harley, Joy Hopping, Angela Shenk Kinser, and Stephanie Wordsmith! And a very special shout-out to Natllerly Roman, one of the sweetest gals I know. You are the true spirits of Christmas present, cheering me on with every page turned and each kind word you've shared with me.

And lastly to my husband, Mark, who has endured a household run on equal parts ink and year-round Christmas music. He has braved the clatter of keys at midnight, the scent of evergreen candles in July to keep me in the holiday spirit, and a few occasional outbursts when the plot just wouldn't behave. God bless him—he's earned it.

Now then, off you go. The season's waiting, the kettle's on, and somewhere yet another book is begging to be read.

Bibliography

A Christmas Carol by Charles Dickens. Heritage Press. 1939.

A Jane Austen Christmas: Regency Christmas Traditions by Maria Grace. White Soup Press. 2014.

Eavesdropping on Jane Austen's England by Roy and Lesley Adkins. Abacus. London. 2014.

Jane Austen Celebrates: Holidays and Occasions Regency Style by Lindy Bell. Day Agency. 2017.

Jane Austen's Table: Recipes Inspired by the Works of Jane Austen by Robert Tuesley Anderson. Thunder Bay Press. 2021.

Stories Behind the Great Traditions of Christmas: Discovering the History of Our Favorite Christmas Celebrations by Ace Collins. Zondervan. 2003.

Street Life in London: People of Victorian England—With Permanent Photographic Illustrations Taken From Life Expressly For This Publication by John Thomson and Adolphe Smith. Omo Press. 2014.

The Time Traveler's Guide to Regency Britain: A Handbook for Visitors to 1789–1830 by Ian Mortimer. Penguin Random House. 2020.

For more from Michelle Griep, read on for an excerpt from

Of Gold and Shadows

In Victorian England, Egyptologist Ami Dalton balances academic life with a covert role rescuing black-market artifacts. Oxford bachelor Edmund Price unexpectedly finds himself entangled with Ami, and as they delve into a newly acquired collection, an artifact rumored to be cursed surfaces, and they wonder if something nefarious is hiding among the shadows.

1

Oxford, England
July 1888

Cemeteries always smelled of earthworms and damp dog fur, especially after a rain, and Brudge rather liked it that way. It made death more tangible. Imminent. An irrefutable reminder that life balanced on a knife's edge. He patted the blade in his coat pocket, the hard lump of it a reassurance that the Shadow Broker wouldn't get the best of him. Not this night. Brudge would be the victor or die in the trying.

"Step smart, Scupper," he called over his shoulder, annoyed that the oaf he hired couldn't keep up with him. To be expected, though, if he really thought on it. A battleship aground wouldn't move with ease, and Scupper was a boatload of muscle and flesh.

Holding his lantern higher, Brudge studied the black shapes in the freshly fallen darkness. Not a particularly brilliant time for a rendezvous, what with the turn of wheels yet grinding along the cobblestones outside the hallowed ground of St. Sepulchre's. Midnight would have been better. Perhaps this Shadow Broker wasn't all he was cracked up to be.

Or it could be a well-calculated appointment to put him at ease before danger cuffed him in the head.

An involuntary shiver spidered down his spine as his gaze shifted left and right. Nothing moved save for the slight tremble of leaves on the trees, dripping leftover raindrops like so many drops of blood. Tombstones the colour of bleached bones popped up from the dirt, quiet sentries of the dead. Nothing out of the ordinary for a graveyard, but he didn't like it. Not a bit. In his line of work, it was the mundane that dulled the senses, and a trafficker of purloined goods ought never give in to passivity. Unless, of course, he didn't mind a gun to the back.

Which he did.

After rounding a bend in the path, Brudge crouched at the next gravestone on the left and squinted.

Beauty, wisdom, fame and wealth
All are stolen by ill-health
Bold or valiant, rugged or brave
None escape the silent grave

What a load of codswallop. Brudge turned aside and spit. If the Shadow Broker thought a few words carved in granite would put the fear of God into him, then the scoundrel clearly didn't know who he was dealing with.

He set the lantern on the ground as instructed in the note he'd received earlier that day. Scupper pulled alongside him, smelling of gardenias of all things. Either the man had a secret penchant, or he still lived with his mother.

"Now what?" Scupper's voice was a foghorn.

"Shsst!" Brudge kept his tone to just above a whisper as he scanned to the far stretches of the light. "No sense letting the whole world know we've arrived."

Scupper had opened his mouth to reply when hardened words hit them both in the back.

"I see you have brought company. That was not part of the deal."

Brudge wheeled about, brows shooting to the clouds as the silhouette of a woman stepped from the shadows of a large tree trunk. She clutched a satchel in each hand, obviously prepared to do business. This slip of a woman was the Shadow Broker? No, it had to be a setup, and a nasty one at that.

"One can never be too cautious," he said, then murmured low to Scupper, "Be on alert." He eased his hand to his pocket, speaking loudly to draw attention to his words instead of the movement. "Had I known you were a skirt, I wouldn't have brought the extra muscle."

"Don't you know you ought not judge a book by its cover, Mr. Brudge?"

He chuckled, ending with a whisper to Scupper, "Check our flank, then circle round and get the goods." Upping his volume, he made a show of clouting the man on the back. "Off you go." Brudge smiled at the woman. "Is that better, miss?"

"There is no need to be condescending." A winter wind blew in her voice, stark against the July evening. "This is not my first purchase."

"So I hear tell." And he had, though he'd give Dandrae the sharp side of his tongue next time he saw him. The cully ought to have warned him the Shadow Broker liked to pull stunts. "How do you wish to play it, then?"

"I should like to inspect the artifact before I give you the money. Set the item down, then back off twenty paces. After I verify the authenticity, I shall put it in this empty satchel." She held up the bag in her left hand. "Then I will leave the money in its place, which is in this one." She lifted the other bag.

Brudge frowned. "Seems only fair I get to do some verifying as well. How do I know you've brought the full amount or even if there's anything in there?"

"In your own words, you have 'heard tell.' So no doubt you know I have never cheated anyone from the agreed-upon price."

A snort ripped out of him. "There's always a first in my line of business."

Though he couldn't see her face, he had no doubt her lips were pinched with irritation. Pulling out a stack of bills, she waved the wad in the air. "Would you like me to count them aloud?"

Sassy little sprite. A grin curved his mouth. "No need."

Shoving his hand into his pocket, he pulled out a cloth-wrapped bundle the length of his palm, hardly two fingers wide, then nestled it atop the gravel. He retreated no more than a step before the woman shot up her palm.

"Take the lantern with you."

He narrowed his eyes. "I thought you said you wanted to inspect the trinket."

Laughter bubbled out of her, more demeaning than humorous. He bristled. He'd never let a man insult him so, much less a woman.

"Just do as you are told, Mr. Brudge."

He snatched up the lantern, the flame casting a wild dance of light as it swung in his grip, then counted off twenty paces. How satisfying it would be when Scupper took this snippet down to the ground.

She approached the tiny parcel, skirts billowing like dark clouds. Setting aside the satchels, she retrieved the package and unwrapped it. Hard to say what she saw in the small figurine. He wouldn't give two coppers for the ugly chunk of clay. Not that it mattered, as long as she was willing to pay.

And since she was, that meant others would part with coins for it too.

Apparently satisfied, she opened the clasp on one bag and tipped it upside down. "As you see, Mr. Brudge, I shall be putting the item into the empty satchel and will leave behind the one with the payment." Like a grand entertainer, she flourished her hand in the air.

Brudge rolled his eyes. How this woman had earned such a shrewd reputation was beyond him. Then again, this could all simply be a charade while the real Shadow Broker hid behind some tombstone. If that was the case, hopefully Scupper could handle him. He'd certainly paid the brute enough.

"Let Mr. Dandrae know if you come across any other Egyptian artifacts. I am always in the market for such." She snapped the bag closed. "Good night, Mr. Brudge. A pleasure doing business with you."

Her skirts swirled as she shot down the gravel path. Brudge ate up the ground himself in a mad dash to grab the money. The clasp broke as he forced the satchel open. Sure enough, a bundle of banknotes sat inside. A slow smile eased across his lips, then broke into a grin as Scupper stepped out of the shadows and grabbed the woman. She'd have screamed were the man's big hand not over her mouth. He wrenched the satchel containing the artifact from her grip just as she elbowed him in the gut, followed by another sharp blow even lower. Scupper grunted.

Brudge winced. That had to hurt.

A curse bellowed out of the man, followed by a swipe of his meat-hook hand. The strike launched the woman sideways. She landed in a heap while Scupper lurched away, hunched over.

Brudge caught up to him and clapped the man on the back. "Good work. Now let's be off. Train leaves in twenty minutes . . . just about the time that chit will wake up with a real skull banger. Stupid woman. She has no business being in a man's world." He chuckled as he clutched both satchels. He could triple the money if he and Scupper pulled this little trick a few more times.

"But keep your eyes keen, eh?" His gaze swept the graveyard like the swing of a scythe. "For all we know, the Shadow Broker might yet be waiting to spring."

A twig in the mouth was as pleasant a sensation as gravel mashed into one's cheek—and a bruised one at that. Stifling a groan, Ami Dalton spit out the small stick, then pushed up to sit. Well. That hadn't gone exactly as planned.

Fingering the soreness in her jaw, she rose on stiff legs. Oh, but a hot soak in a rose-scented bath would be a welcome diversion this night. With quick sweeps of her hands, she dusted herself off, then glowered at a large tear in her hem. Must bullies always use force to get what they wanted? Then again, in order to bring history to life for the masses, one must be willing to face danger now and then—or so her father always said.

She huffed a disgusted puff of air as she picked her way through the maze of tombstones. The rear gate, while out of the way, was the safer route if Mr. Brudge and his hammer man came back. A beauty of a headache pounded in her temple as she upped her pace. Mr. Dandrae should have investigated this pair more thoroughly before suggesting she work with them. Such slipshod connections weren't like him . . . unless he'd taken a larger-than-usual cut of the profits. Possible. He was a consummate businessman even if his dealings were sometimes on the wrong side of the law. Perhaps Mr. Brudge had paid him too handsomely to refuse, or perhaps the man owned a little dirt on Mr. Dandrae. Regardless, Mr. Dandrae would hear of the heavy-handed horseplay that'd gone on tonight and make sure it didn't happen again, or she'd pull her business from him.

Hinges screeched like demons in the night as she opened the cemetery gate. Ahead sat a black cab with an even blacker horse hitched to it. The animal pawed the ground, a massive snort misting from his nostrils in the glow of the coach's lanterns.

"Ready to leave, miss?" the driver called from his seat.

"Yes, please." She boarded, taking care to tuck in her gown before shutting the door. No sense adding tear upon tear to the already battered fabric.

Sinking against the seat, she nearly closed her eyes. Yet no. This was a time not for rest but for celebration. With one quick movement, she pulled out the small bundle she'd jammed up her sleeve, then unwrapped the ancient shabti doll, the same shape and size of the rock she'd left inside the satchel Mr. Brudge stole. Mr. Clampstone would bounce on his toes when he got his hands on this gem. Another prize for the Ashmolean Museum's Egyptian collection and another step forward in her career to becoming a recognized Egyptologist. After six months of her identifying and acquiring unique pieces, Mr. Clampstone ought to be offering her that part-time Egyptologist position any day now. Which would be a boon. And yet even with such a title, she'd still be nowhere near gaining a smidgeon of the respect her father enjoyed. She'd never become a team member on an Egyptian dig without such respect. A sigh leaked out of her.

But even so, she smiled as she rewrapped the precious relic. If nothing else, the Shadow Broker had maintained her reputation, and for now, that would have to be enough.

Michelle Griep has been writing since she first discovered blank wall space and Crayola. She is a Christy Award–winning author of historical romances that both intrigue and evoke a smile. She's an Anglophile at heart, and you'll most often find her partaking of a proper cream tea while scheming up her next novel . . . but it's probably easier to find her at MichelleGriep.com or on Facebook, Instagram, and Pinterest.

Sign Up for Michelle's Newsletter

Keep up to date with Michelle's latest news on book releases and events by signing up for her email list at the link below.

MichelleGriep.com

FOLLOW MICHELLE ON SOCIAL MEDIA

Michelle Griep

@MichelleGriep

@MichelleGriep